The Ringmaster of My Creative Imagination

GUILLERMO F. PORRO III

The Ringmaster of My Creative Imagination

For information about this title or to order other books and/or electronic media, contact:

Guillermo Porro
dadeshark19@yahoo.com

ISBN: 978-1-087-84163-2 Paperback

Printed in the United States of America
Cover and Interior Design: Infinity Flower Publishing, LLC

For those with creative spirits - the world will try to set you to its standards, but it's your job to design a different landscape.

- Guillermo F. Porro III

Something Different

Behind every creative mind plays the instruments of an orchestra. Everything broken into sections, yet together; it's something magical. Now the question is, what exactly goes into creating a story? Like, is it just sitting behind a keyboard and letting your head roam free? Sending it into different worlds, behind the views of a race you just thought of?

Before your eyes appears a person for this story, a male. His eyes are a natural blue shade, sitting beneath brown curls which sprout like weeds. His name is Guillermo, and he is a creative guy in a world built for the mechanical. Yet here he sits in front of a flashing screen, empty of words and punctuation. Now, Guillermo has written before; in fact, completed stories and poems alike. However, he blinks as a faint smell of smoke fills the room as the gears in his head grind away. See, I know this because I am his inner-self, and the narrator for this beautiful journey.

If you look carefully, you can see me kicking my feet in the open air as Guillermo scratches his head. Looking over and seeing the blank expression forces me to get up onto my feet. I make my way from his shoulder, toward his neck, before approaching the side of his head. Shaking my head, I push the strands of hair aside, revealing the porous, pale skin behind it. Before heading any further, I look down at Guillermo's fingers, which continue to hover aimlessly above the keyboard. I turn back and step through the epidermis wall before disappearing from the outside room. Things go dark as lights bolt past me from all sides, colors brightening and fading. After a momentary sensation of queasiness, a flashing light appears in front of me with a single word written on it.

"Imagination," I read aloud, feeling a glow swell inside my cheeks.

See, imagination is the hub for all the insanity that is created by one's mind. I mean dragons, robots, magic, just to name a few, is all created within this space. It's not easy, believe me, I have seen countless stories grow to become written and some have the potential of something magnificent only to dud out.

My feet land onto a floor of thoughts intertwining themselves about. Sections glow one piece at a time, eventually stopping at the other end. All around, the walls rumble as they shoot outwards, revealing a much more significant space. It is kind of intimidating; making it worse is the darkness swallowing up the mass. The only lights are the chain of thoughts which continue to trek around, allowing me to follow at a safe distance.

After a couple of steps, a bright light erupts from the darkness, revealing an archway just out of reach. I duck my head inside seeing the very center of Guillermo's imagination. To outsiders, it is a circus, with random ideas just floating at will. However, to those with much more experience, we merely appreciate the beauty of a story in the process. I mean, it's so cool to watch a single strain of thought become a sentence, and then something so much more.

Making my way through the fluctuating lights, I watch as they turn upwards, bringing normalcy to the space. For a moment, the thoughts remain still, allowing me to catch a glimpse of the developing thoughts. From left to right, rings dig themselves down into the darkness when a spotlight shoots down. Landing, the light channels itself onto a platform in the center. As I move closer, I see a figure in bright colors from head to toe pose. A large top hat hangs between his fingers.

Before I get too close, he places it on top of his rebellious brown locks. Once it settles, the man lifts his hand, causing the darkness to roll away. I watch as row after row of imaginary audiences appears from behind curtains. Sitting in silence, I turn back to see the man drop down from his platform. He comes closer, each step leaving a glittery footprint, until he stops on the brink of the darkness. He then turns back to look at the shining light remaining on the platform. He snaps his fingers, causing the light to flicker before shifting its beam to the his new location. I can see clearly his bright red jacket over a yellow shirt.

"Who are you?" I ask, allowing my eyes time to take him in.

"The name is Ringmaster Periwinkle," he replies, shifting his hat over to the side. Suddenly, the audience roars with applause, causing me to step back as his eyes glimmer in excitement.

I feel a tingle in my throat when the crowd drops their noise to a whisper, returning us back into silence. Behind Periwinkle, the three rings start to shine, the colors glistening. Each ring shoots up, swirling upwards into the ceiling. My gaze shifts to Periwinkle as he starts to shift his shoulders back and forth.

"What are you doing?" I ask in confusion.

"Don't you hear the music?" Periwinkle asks back, stopping suddenly.

I shake my head, causing the smile on Periwinkle's face to drop to a simple smirk.

"Close your eyes," Periwinkle says.

After a moment of hesitation, I shut my eyes, beginning to hear the faint sounds of a marching band filtering through my ears. With each drumline, the music is louder and I snap open my eyes, expecting to see a band in front of me. Instead, I see Periwinkle moving his shoulders and tapping his feet. Then, just before he can drop his foot again, the music comes to a screeching halt.

"What happened?" I ask, waiting for the music to start again.

Before he can answer, an enormous block drops down on top of the three rings, sending shockwaves across the arena floor. We both look back to see it just sitting there, silence filling the room. I realize the audience is gone, as the whispers have gone silent.

"The worst part of being creative," replies Periwinkle in a solemn tone.

"Which is?" I ask.

"Writer's block," replies Periwinkle.

"How bad can that be?" I ask, looking back over to the giant block.

"It can snuff out any act of brilliance if not destroyed," replies Periwinkle. A mallet suddenly appears in his hand, so cartoonish that even streamers hang from the handle. Periwinkle skips his way over to the block, his mallet bouncing off the ground.

Standing before the block, Periwinkle kneels and wraps his hand around part of it, getting a feel for the texture. He squeezes it, watching as the material molds around his fingers. Periwinkle then looks back at me with a sick look on his face as he releases the material.

"What is it?" I ask, watching Periwinkle shake the final bits from his palm.

"Paper Mache," replies Periwinkle, looking down as the material begins to form into a perfect swan.

He shifts his gaze onto the big block. Tightening his grip around the mallet, Periwinkle slowly brings the weapon within inches of its surface. I feel anticipation swell within my chest as I watch him pull back and size up his swing. Then, before I can react, Periwinkle swings it into the surface, causing fragments of paper to shred all over. As the remnants flutter through the air innocently, Periwinkle looks over to admire his strength. From within a dark shell, light begins to stream outwards, a quiet rumble echoing off the walls. Periwinkle takes a step closer and gazes into the opening before stepping back. He then looks back at me with a tremendous smile from ear to ear.

"What is it?" I ask with a slight bit of fear.

"INSPIRATION!" roars Periwinkle. Then with a thunderous strike, Periwinkle lands a blow into the center of the crackling surface. An explosion of random letters and words erupts from the opening. As they shoot through the air, Periwinkle wipes the paper from his face. He then turns toward me so that I can see the ink smudges on his face.

"You might want to wipe off your face," I say, watching him look up into the darkness.

Before my eyes, water rains down upon him, drenching him from head to toe. As the water disappears, Periwinkle runs his hand through his hair, revealing his face. Not a trace of the ink remains as he grins.

A light attracts our attention to the crumbling block, showing a landscape on the other side. I walk up next to Periwinkle, catching sight of the bright colors and shifting lines. Before either of us can speak, the block collapses into bright specks of light, allowing us to fully take in the beauty.

Before our eyes, the struggling rings are exploding with energy and color as the world around them shines with light. Above us, flowing colorful fabric sways freely, the crowd suddenly roaring all around. It is indeed a circus, except inside each of the three rings sits a single door.

My eyes catch sight of the one farthest to the left as I watch clowns of all sizes sit down around it. One by one, chairs appear, allowing the clowns to sit. Their makeup suddenly fades from view, revealing their true nature underneath. From out of thin air, desks surround them, along with pen and journals in front of them. They pick up their pens and turn their focus toward the blank pages.

"What are they doing? I ask, as suddenly the space goes dark, leaving the spotlight on us.

"Preparing one of the one-hunderd poems he has written," replies Periwinkle, slinking away into the darkness.

Before I can search for him, Periwinkle reappears inside the large ring in dim light. The cheers fade away, returning the silence as the large ring slides closer. I watch as the ring slides within inches of my feet. Above, the lights begin to brighten again. Periwinkle stares at me.

"How does this help him build a story?" I ask, motioning to all the things that had just happened.

Periwinkle grins before turning around to a small pathway between the rows of writers. Without a reply, he dashes through them, ruffling the papers and causing them to grumble under their breaths. Before long, he stops in front of the shut door and turns back to me.

"Every story has to start somewhere," Periwinkle replies. He then pushes the door open. As the door swings wider, it reveals a hallway with walls beyond the doorframe with a plain white tile flooring leading the way.

My eyes shift to Periwinkle as I, too, begin my trek through the writers. After I step into the center of the circle, a hand reaches out to block my path forward. Stopping, I turn to see the remnants of clown tears remaining on a tan face. I look into his brown eyes which well up with tears. "What's wrong?"

"I need a word that rhymes with classic," the writer whispers.

"Magic," I whisper back.

I watch his face light up as the tears dry. He looks back to the blank page and attempts to write down whatever inspiration I had given. Before I can see his writing, I notice Periwinkle flailing his arms around like a fish out of water. He nods his head in the direction of the door, forcing me to give up sticking around and head his way. With each step, the space behind me darkens, leaving a bright path in front of me. Just as I get to the open door, I stop and look over at Periwinkle.

"You want to see what he came up with don't you?" Periwinkle asks. I nod gently as Periwinkle lifts one of his hands into the air. A sheet of paper flutters into his grasp. He lowers it and hands it off to me. Grabbing hold, my eyes shift toward two lines of writing on the notebook paper.

"Some kinds of love even at this age can be classic," I read aloud.

"That walking hand in hand on the beach makes magic," adds Periwinkle.

My eyes pass over the second line, taking in the the words . I then look up to find his toothy grin as he points to the door once more. Quickly folding the paper, I take a couple of steps toward the door. I stop just shy of the outer frame and poke my head into space. Before me, a large hallway heads into infinity with doors lining both sides. Each was a different color, brightening the monotony of the bare walls.

"What is this place?" I ask.

"The Creative History of Guillermo," replies Periwinkle.

My eyes shift back as I step into the room. Behind me, a shadow creeps inside as I hear the door close. Periwinkle walks around me to take the lead as I continue to take in these new surroundings. It was straight and narrow with a slight glow coming from beneath the doors. I wonder about the source of light and the imagination, sitting, waiting for Guillermo to open. I find the thought hypnotizing as I approach a door. Without a thought, my hand reaches for the doorknob, attempting to twist it open.

My wonder shatters when the door doesn't budge, forcing me to return to reality. My eyes drop to the doorknob, finding not even an opening for any sort of key. Before I can speak, thunderous pounding roars from the backside of the door. I lean in to catch the sounds of explosions and lightning crashing about. My attention shifts to Periwinkle as he makes his way in front of me.

"What is behind these doors?" I ask him.

"Past experiences," replies Periwinkle.

"Why are they locked?" I ask him, standing up straight.

"They are here only for when Guillermo needs them to write," replies Periwinkle, taking a look at the line of doors ahead of us. He takes a couple of steps before stopping in the middle of the hallway. Periwinkle lifts his hand up in the air and begins to move is in a wiping motion, back and forth. I watch as the hallway smears away before revealing a massive door connecting the two sides. Slowly, I make my way forward as Periwinkle looks back at me with a grin.

"How did you do that?" I ask.

"I'm the ringmaster," replies Periwinkle, turning back as a doorknob appears in front of his hand. I watch his hand hover over the doorknob before he pulls it away.

"What is it?" I ask him, beginning to make my way over to him. The door grows in quality, revealing the grains in the wood among the shiny metal around the knob.

"This is where I leave you for now," replies Periwinkle. He steps back, into the wall, before merging with it. I watch helplessly as he disappears from my sight, leaving me alone in front of the door.

I take a couple steps, nervous as I focus on the door. It is high above my head, even though the doorknob remains at my level. I extend my hand to find the knob giving as it quickly turns to the left. With a single push, the door swings open, allowing me to step inside. My eyes widen in surprise when I find myself inside a room with no features at all.

No doors or windows, just a circular room with a ring of carpet surrounding a section of white tiles. Gazing around, I watch as the floor in the center suddenly disappears beneath the carpeting. A golden circle begins to lift from the ground, revealing bars draping toward another flat piece. It rises all the way to the roof. The gold shine blinds me as I try to take in the individual rods of gold surrounding the two flat pieces. A massive trunk of wood lies horizontally within it.

I am surprised when a creature jumps on top of it, black feathers covering its body. I manage to make it out its charcoal eyes behind its beak, which slightly curves to allow the beast to get a better look.

Remaining silent, I watch the creature open its wings as its tail feathers hang off the other side. I take a couple of steps to the side, watching it follow me silently with its eyes. I then try to move to the other side, watching it follow me there.

"What are you doing?" the creature says.

"Trying to figure out what you are," I reply, watching its head tilt to one side.

"You could just ask," the creature says.

"Who are you?" I ask.

"My name is Edalpo, and I'm the guardian of this room," Edalpo says, retracting his wings around his feathery body. This creature is only something I had read about in Guillermo's favorite story. However, this one seems a bit confused as his eyes flit around the room. He surprises me when he spins around in search of something.

"What are you looking for?" I ask, watching as he turns his beak back and forth.

"Doors," replies Edalpo.

Suddenly, the golden bars dissipate and lift into the sky, forming a swirling cloud above. Edalpo and I look up in time to watch crackling, golden lightning bolts strike the walls. With each impact, golden divots remain, causing a gold liquid to cascade down the walls. The fluid begins to gather, forming a solid mass. It solidifies, becoming stable on the wall. To my surprise, around the room, three rectangular shapes appear on the wall. Not a drop of the liquid lands anywhere on the carpet.

I look over to find no trace of the ravenesque creature before returning my focus to the golden rectangles. I slowly approach the first one, examining it as I grow closer to it. At first, no features stand out, but then a handprint begins to form. I reach out and place my hand firmly within the print, watching as it begins to glow, before suddenly crumbling to the ground, leaving golden chunks across the floor. Kicking a couple of pieces off my feet, I look up to find a closet-sized room, a mirrored surface reflecting back at me. The reflection gets larger as I make my way inside, darkens surrounding me.

Inside, I gaze upon the mirror, seeing my reflection distort into two separate images. Taking shape, two faces are revealed, with features similar to Guillermo's. One is a balding man with a pair of caring, brown eyes above a goatee of salt and pepper hair. Next to him is another man, very different but still much like the first. A large mop of black hair rises above his wire glasses and a dark brown cigar is between his lips. I don't have long to ponder them as another figure begins to take shape, a female face quite similar to Guillermo's. Motherly from hair to chin, yet so alike this face was to Guillermo's own, that I begin to smile at the entire portrait.

"I see you found the first significant inspiration for his writing," replies a voice.

I turn to see Periwinkle behind me, standing tall with his hands behind his back.

"What is that?" I ask, turning my attention back to the motionless faces.

Without a reply, Periwinkle steps past me to look at the faces in the mirror for a moment. He then turns back, looking at me, before turning back to them. With half a smirk, Periwinkle snaps his fingers, causing the faces to swirl away. "Follow me."

"Where?" I ask, watching as he turns toward the exit.

He pauses in the doorway, placing his hand on the golden frame. "To the next inspiration." Before I can reply, Periwinkle continues out into the main room.

I watch him turn to the left and head toward the next door while I momentarily stop just outside the doorway. I turn back to see my faint reflection in the mirror, when suddenly the golden door swings shut. Shifting my attention from the glistening surface, I find Periwinkle a step away from the next door. "Can you open them too?"

"Of course! I'm the ringleader in this imagination circus," Periwinkle replies, snapping his fingers once more. This time, the golden surface slides out of the way and reveals a dirty tile floor.

I step closer, unsure of this next door, surprised when I find myself alone in a massive room. Rows of seating appear from the front to the back, completely empty, as a stage lifts up from the front of the room. On top of it, a band appears, instruments in hand as they begin to play an opening harmony. Their melody pulses in waves through the entire room as a single cross appears on each wall with a single projection behind the musicians.

The word Passion appears in a chorus of lights, a shadows suddenly stepping from between the bandmates. To my surprise, it was a heart with hands, but no arms attaching them to the organ tissue. In one of its hands, the heart carries a metallic pole, from which an all-white flag waves gently. The heart grabs hold of the mic stand that appears at the edge of the stage and begins to sing out lyrics to the song. My chest tightens as I listen to the words of the song, feeling a tear making its way toward my chin. I quickly wipe it off when I catch sight of a pair of beings.

A sudden, invisible force pulls me toward them, sitting me down behind the two figures. As the song continues, I hear one of the beings struggling to not allow the emotion to overwhelm him. He suddenly erupts from his seat, standing at attention as the heart sings the second chorus.

Before too long, the figure next to him, a female, stands at his side and places her hand on his shoulder. I watch as his tears drip from his jaw, when suddenly the tune fades away along with the band. From out of the empty stage, a bright light explodes, sending waves into the rest of the room. Within my chest, I feel the emotion dissipate, leaving nothing but a sense of relief.

In front of me, the female figure disappears, leaving the male by himself. Listening carefully, I hear the man mumbling incoherently before he too vanishes. Now alone, I look around to find the room completely empty before a shadow begins to appear. I jerk my head back, realizing it's Periwinkle. He makes his way down the aisle, tapping the tops of the seats of each row.

Spotting me, Periwinkle pauses at the end of my row. Without a word, he sits down in the empty chair next to me. "What inspiration is this?" I ask quietly.

"Faith," Periwinkle replies simply.

"All I saw was tears and a bright light," I reply, looking over at the empty stage on the other end of the room.

"On the outside, yes, but on the inside, he felt an enormous relief from all the pain at the moment," replies Periwinkle. Before I can respond, Periwinkle points toward the stage. The figure resembling Guillermo is kneeling beside the steps, his head down on his hands, silent as we whisper in the back of the room.

"How does this inspire him?" I ask, sitting forward in the chair.

"It gave him a focus for his turbulent emotions," Periwinkle says, standing up.

Silently, I stand up next to him as he makes his way back out into the aisle. Following in his footsteps, we make our way back toward the doorway. As Periwinkle disappears into the light beyond the door, I stop and turn back to see the figure still kneeling.

All of a sudden, its head lifts up toward the white ceiling before returning its eyes back down to the floor. Sadness fills me, but I push it away as I turn my head to the light and step through.

I find myself within the walls of the circular room. Behind me, the golden door closes like the one previous, leaving no way to return. All that is left is the final door, the last source of inspiration behind the writing that Guillermo creates.

From outside my sight, Edalpo swoops in and lands down on a lone branch sticking out of the wall. He squeezes his claws together, causing the branch to angle downward. Suddenly, the final golden door swings open, revealing a mixture of darkness and light as it enters the room. Edalpo looks in and shivers before taking off out of view, leaving me alone once more.

I stare hard at the door as I take heavy steps toward it. I pause in the opening, peeking my head beyond the golden frame. I jump back when a bolt of lightning cracks the open sky. After a small rumble, torrential rain roars down from above, drenching me as I step inside.

The ground transforms into swaying grass as far as the eye can see on both sides of a hill. From out of the ground, sections drop down, revealing holes within the dirt. The ground rumbles as tombstones rise from the ground in front of each hole. Once they stop moving, the holes fill up, leaving just a single hole open in front of me. After a couple of steps through the soggy grass, I stand next to the opening. Looking at the tombstone, my eyes take in the drops of rain falling toward the ground, the tombstone bare and smooth without any writing. It was awaiting something or someone, but whom, I wondered, until suddenly writing began to form. Letter by letter, the wording appears before my eyes.

"Mortality," a voice says simply, making me jump. I step back and look around, trying to find the source of the voice, instead finding nothing but thick rain and darkness.

Suddenly something catches my attention. One by one, a single word is etched into the tombstones as another lightning bolt strikes down into the gaping hole in front of me. The blast shoots me back into another headstone, fracturing it into pieces. Shaking off the shock, I look toward the smoldering opening, seeing smoke swirl out of it as thunder rumbles around me.

I realize the smoke is fading as the rain weakens into a slight drizzle before stopping altogether, leaving just puddles and a sparkling coating on the various surfaces. Suddenly, the sky goes clear, revealing a blanket of stars. The momentary peace is shattered as a shadowy figure rises from the hole.

Its ominous aura darkens the entire space as it steps out onto the ground in front of me. As its foot lands on the grass, the blades turn brown, before wilting away before as it lifts its foot. With each step, I feel my chest tighten with anticipation, the faint moonlight failing to reveal the being under the dark hood. It came toward me silently, almost as if it didn't even see me, until it stopped directly in front of me. I watched in fear as it lifted its hands toward the hood and pushed it away. I exhaled hard, recognizing the face of a familiar ringmaster.

"Were you scared?" Periwinkle asks with a grin, pulling back the sleeves to reveal skeletal hands. My eyes widen at the sight before he then pulls them off and throws them into the hole behind him.

"For being a figment of Guillermo, I was indeed," I reply, my body relaxing.

Periwinkle looks at me as his hands appear in the long sleeves. He waves one, his hat appearing. He places it on top of his head and adjusts it to fit perfectly. "Have you seen the final motivation for his writing?"

My eyes wander around the cemetary before once more reading the word on the face of the tombstone. "Mortality?" I reply with uncertainty.

As Periwinkle's face glows with happiness, the sky above lightens, revealing a gorgeous sun among the sparse clouds. With no words, Periwinkle nods his head, forcing me to try to understand the meaning. All around, the scenery lightens up, providing a new scene. The grass turns green as vines tangle around the bare tombstones. Drifting away, the clouds float off to the horizon as I struggle to comprehend. I look over at Periwinkle, who has made his way over to the edge of the open grave. "What are you doing?"

Periwinkle flicks his finger and motions me toward him. I approach him as he points his finger down into the hole. Gazing down into the darkness of the hole, I see nothing, not even a glimmer of light in the darkness. The walls seem to absorb the light from the sun above us. Before I can question him, Periwinkle kicks a couple of pebbles into the opening. Following their trajectory, I watch in surprise as the pebbles disappear into the space without a sound, as if they kept falling beyond our sight.

"What is down there?" I ask, looking up to Periwinkle.

He grins and a slight twinkle appears in his eyes. "A movie theatre."

Now, having only seen said movie theatre through the Guillermo's eyes, I can only imagine what exactly that is. As far as I can remember, it is a place to go and see videos filled with storyline and character development. A place that Guillermo didn't really enjoy because he would always think of things he would add to make it his own. "Why a movie theatre?"

"Despite his unquenchable imagination, Guillermo always wondered what some of his stories would look like," Periwinkle replies.

"I get that, but why are they inside a grave?" I ask.

"These are his projects that never saw the light of day," Periwnkle replies. Before I can reply, he lifts up into the air and then disappears within the darkness of the grave. The silence returns, allowing the swirling winds to return as tumbling leaves land all around. After a couple moments, the blue sky suddenly darkens with a rumble of thunder.

"Brain storm," I murmur before stepping off into the darkness.

My eyes turn from the bright sky above toward the entrapping darkness. Once inside, the I search desperately for a sign of light in the darkness. Then I saw it, a single bead of light beneath me, beginning to grow in leaps and bounds. It took my attention as I forgot that I was still falling, even though it felt as if I was not even moving. Plummeting into the light, colors begin to appear and textures form all around me. Suddenly, the light pulls back and my feet crash into solid ground, sending a jolt up my frame. My eyes shut momentarily as the ringing in my ears begins to fade.

"Welcome to Imagination Cinema," a voice calls through the ringing.

I look up to see Periwinkle back in his colorful threads and rid of the deathly robe. Around us, dull walls surround us as caution tape drapes from all angles. The roof struggles to hold onto its tiles, and flickering lights allow us moments of guidance through the drearyness. Moldy carpet sinks beneath me feet and I look up, noticing a certain glittery figure disappear out of sight. "Periwinkle?"

"Yes?" he calls.

Before my eyes can make their way around the room, a figure steps out from the shadows, wearing a worn tuxedo. Interestingly enough, he actually blends in with the surroundings rather than being at the forefront. His usual top hat is gone, with an old-fashioned dress hat in its place. A red ribbon wraps around it as his brown hair tries to escape from beneath it. He takes a couple steps toward me before manifesting a black and white walking cane. "Is that you?"

"It is," Periwinkle replies, bowing at his knees.

"Why have you brought me here?" I ask, continuing to look around.

"To show you that every great achievement doesn't come with setbacks," Periwinkle replies, twirling his cane in his hand. After a final spin, the cane extends away from us and down the hall.

"What do you mean by setbacks?" I ask.

"Loss of inspiration," Periwinkle replies.

Suddenly, the colors disappear from the room causing everything to fade. Before I can speak, he turns around and watches as the entire hall clears out, allowing us free movement. After turning back with a slight grin, he starts to walk down the hall, leaving me alone. After a moment, he looks back, finding me still in the same spot, my eyes following the moulding of the wall. I stop, feeling his stare as

I turn toward him. Placing one foot in front of the other, my steps quicken, closing the gap between us.

"Sorry about that," I say, taking another step closer.

"It's okay, Guillermo has that attention thing too," Periwinkle replies with a shrug. He then turns back around and continues down the hall with me in toe. For a moment, I felt like I was his shadow, until he stopped and I walked through him.

My eyes widen as I look back at Periwinkle, who looks unfazed at my action. Instead, he turns his attention to a single brown door that stands before him. With a flick of the wrist, he opens the door and reveals the space behind it. The space darkens as Periwinkle looks over at me.

"Let's watch a movie," Periwinkle replies. He then steps into the dark space as I watch.

After he disappears, I step forward into the darkness, finding myself at the edge of a tiny staircase. Beyond the stairs are two dark leather chairs facing in the direction of a massive screen. Behind the chairs is a projector sitting on top of a large stand which connects to the carpeting below. In the farthest chair, Periwinkle sits with his cane off to his side.

"What, no popcorn?" I ask, taking the two steps down.

Periwinkle looks over to the left and watches as a table lifts from the ground with a massive bag of popcorn oozing with butter. He then turns back to the blank screen as I make my over to the other chair.

As I take a seat, Periwinkle reaches between the chair and the wall, pulling a remote from out of the sight. "Are you ready for the first short film?"

"What is it about?" I reply.

"Elements and brotherly love," Periwinkle says, clicking the green on top of the control.

"Sounds interesting," I reply, watching the dark screen light up.

As the particles make their way from the buzzing projector, the image on the screen begins to focus. After a moment to adjust, a giant number three extends from the top to the bottom. A whistling sound interupts the buzzing sound as a countdown begins on the screen. Suddenly it disappears before images of human beings and a landscape appear in frame.

"Let us start the show," Periwinkle says as the figures begin to move about.

My eyes shift toward the screen to watch the changing images. Person by person, rows of human figures appear, sitting upon chairs in a room of some sort. Suddenly, the view shifts from third to first person when it focuses in on a singular student, a textbook in front of him. To his left, a window with a layer of moisture growing ever so slightly blocks the scenery outside. We watch as the focus shifts behind him as a narrator's voice starts to crackle from the speakers around us:

The First Film

The window, a guiding light to potential, or a teaser of what is to come.

This is what I stare out of every day, from this desk that keeps me down. As the voices all around me try to talk over my thoughts, I still think of nothing but creative freedom. A place where my mind roams free and makes magical places all day long; where my words bring images to an audience, who sees what I can imagine.

Oh well, I guess that might never come, since I'm stuck here in this desk. My name is Walter Turner, and I am an average student here at this school. I can see the brown of my eyes and hair reflecting in the window as my teacher approaches my desk. I turn to see her angry face, and her hand points out to the front door. As a breath sinks into my lungs, I lift myself to the whispers of my classmates. I slowly make my way to the end of the row of desks, seeing my one friend, Ralph, shaking his head.

I continue into the corridor as the door shuts behind me with a small slam. I stop right outside and look up and down the hall, lockers lining the walls in both directions, a pastey-white tile floor between them. The roof, a yellowish shade of white, goes as far as my eyes can see, with an occasional light fixture hanging down. This is truly no setting for a mind like my own.

However, it is my figurative prison borne from the uncreative minds that surround me: the ones that give you a code on how to dress and when to get to places. After walking for a moment, I found a familiar door. Step by step, I pass by the old lockers with their shiny locks until finally, I stand before the door labeled, in bright red letters, Main Office. I gulp down a breath, for behind this door is a creature that sends a chill down every student's spine.

"Principal's office, here I come again," I whisper, reaching out for the door handle.

Just as I go to turn it, suddenly the lights flicker down the hall. I pull my hand back and look around. Surprised, I realize I hear the sound of footsteps and I see a shadow looming around a corner. Fear fills me as the large shadow shrinks down, and Ralph turns the corner. His giant smile from ear to ear eases the monotony.

"They should give you VIP sitting in there," he chuckles as he comes to a stop in front of me.

I let out a laugh. "Maybe the same day you tell your crush how you feel about her," I reply, which causes Ralph to stop in his tracks. His pale cheeks turn rose-red and he looks over to one of the classroom doors nearby.

"I'm too chicken for that," he mumbles.

I place my hand on his shoulder, and grin before he can knock it off. "Good luck with that," I reply.

Ralph gives a thumbs-up as his eyes lift over my shoulder to the door behind me.

"Yeah, you too," he says before turning down the hallway.

Once more, I gulp in fear as I turn back to the door. Once again, the menacing door stood in front of me with light escaping around its frame from inside. It's almost like the sun is trying to escape, except it can't 'cause there's no joy in a place like this. My hand shakes as I slowly reach for the cold, metal handle.

A chill shoots up my arm when my hand grabs hold of it. I close my eyes briefly as I push on the handle, feeling the mechanism unlock. The door swings outwards, which allows the bright light to escape. After a moment of blindness, my sight returns to take in the familiar office. The usual rusty chairs sit alongside one wall, while on the other end is a counter the same color as a tree. Behind that, I spot the office aide at her desk, her face hiding behind a curtain of blonde hair.

"Afternoon," I blurt out, causing her to turn to me.

Her face is a mixture of emotion as she looks at me before she stands up from her office chair, clearly annoyed and not surprised to see me. She then steps from behind the counter and leans her elbow on it.

"Well, if it isn't Walter Turner," the she snarks.

Before I can reply with something witty, she pulls out a folder with a couple sheets of paper on top. Then, she reaches for a blue pen and writes down something. Before I can question her, from behind me a door creaks open, catching my attention. I watch as a gentleman of a fair complexion appears, his dark suit matching all the way down to his shoes, except for a red tie. I look at his face just in time to see him frown.

"Come in Walter," the man says.

"Yes, Principal Miller," I reply as I head to the doorway.

He steps to the side to allow me into his dimly lit office. From behind me, I hear him speak to the aide, "Mrs. Jones, please call the parents."

My heart drops in my chest and my eyes begin to redden as my emotions sour. I can hear her pick up the phone and dial the keypad.

"Hello, is this Walter's mom?" she asks, her voice fading as the principal closes the door.

I find myself in one of the worst places someone my age can be. The principal's office seems to be the darkest room in the entire school, even with a massive window hidden behind a giant oak desk. The principal makes his way between the desk and the window and sits in a giant leather chair. I turn back around momentarily, straining to hear the aide on the phone, but unable to hear anything clearly. I suck in the deepest breath I can, turning back to see Principal Miller's stoic posture, a three-ringed folder open on his desk.

"Please sit," he instructs.

I gently nod spotting a chair near the wall. My feet feel heavy as I make my way over and lift it off the ground. I will admit, this time I felt like throwing it out the window and jumping after it. However, I place the chair down onto the marble floor and take a seat in front of the desk. Before he speaks, he draws a deep breath, which causes his nostrils to flare. He turns to open a side drawer and picks up a pen from out of its depths.

"Walter, you have been in here more often than I like to remember," the principal says.

I remain quiet while I watch as his eyes target me. *Have I really been in here that much?* I thought to myself. Just before words slip between my lips, the door behind me swings open rather hard, making me jump. I look back to see the aide in the doorway.

"The parents are on their way," she says.

I feel my world crashing down around me. My heart drops to my stomach and the color fades from my face. I slowly look over to the principal, who remains stern in his chair.

"So, Walter, it appears to your teachers that you have been dozing off in class," he says.

My mind races as I try to come up with a good excuse. *A.D.D.or something*, I thought, *that would be good.* However, I know he won't believe that.

"I merely like to appreciate nature's beauty," I reply innocently.

He leans back, almost taken back by my honesty. He then sits forward before he reaches down to the folder on his desk. He opens it, revealing the stack of papers inside. After he shuffles the line, he pulls a couple out, held together with a shiny staple. He closes the fold and lays the papers on top. He flips the top page over, which reveals to me a report of some sort. It lands softly on the wooden top as he begins to read the page in front of him.

"Creative…amazing…excellent word choice," he says as he keeps his eyes down on the paper.

With each word, I nod at their positivity, watching as he lifts the top page over. He then reaches down, and picks it up by the sides before he turns it around. I look at the cover, reading the words. After my eyes read the last word, I lean back in the chair. He drops the report back onto the desk and looks at me.

"Am I in trouble?" I ask.

He snickers, to my surprise. Usually, he became red in the face. This time was different though; I didn't know why at first.

"You are being suspended," he replies.

That last word struck me in the chest like a ton of bricks. I could not understand why I'd be suspended for merely zoning out because class bores me. After a moment, reality sank in, and I drop my head on to my lap. Before I can even think about what I could have replied with, my throat shuts and my brain freezes.

Great, now my words fail me, I think to myself.

"Take this time as project time," he continues.

Suddenly, my thoughts shift from negative to curious. "What do you mean by project time?"

He opens his desk drawer once more, and pulls out a paper. He lays it out in front of me to allow me to skim it.

"Writing contest for all schools in District 1986, to promote the rejuvenation of arts," I read aloud.

"What do you think?" he asks.

"I mean, it could be a challenge. Is there no one else that can do it?" I reply as I try to come up with an idea.

"Not that I have seen, and besides, you seem to be the student for the job," he says.

I can feel a warm glow from my cheeks. My ego went from flat one second, to suddenly overgrown in another. "What about my grades?" I ask. Not sure why I was concerned about them, but I was sure my parents would.

"This will count for the assignments you miss, as an agreement with your teachers," he replies.

Before another word can be spoken, the doorknob twists open. My mom and dad step into the room with confusion on their faces. I turn around as the principal sits back in his chair.

"What did he do now?" my dad asks angrily.

The principal sits forward once again. "Sorry for the confusion, but the answer is nothing bad," he replies.

I watch as the anger fades away, and that familiar look of confusion came over them. They plant themselves on either side of me, placing their hands on my shoulders.

"So why were we called down here?" my mom asks.

The principal lowers his eyes to the desk, and picks up the report. He then hands it across the desk to my dad. He takes the paper, looking down at it.

"Desean Dubois and the Art of Photography," my dad says. That was the title of my original report from a few years back. It was about a man named Desean, who used photography to show people the beauty in little things.

"Indeed, and this is the most creatively written piece of work I have seen," the principal says.

"Okay, but your aide said he was suspended," my mom adds. She is always direct, and wants to get to the point of matters.

"I'm sorry my aide used that term, I meant for her to tell you that your son is going to be doing some work from home," the principal replies.

"Like homework?" my dad asks.

"Sort of, this work is more for the benefit of the school," the principal replies.

"How will this affect his grades?" my mom asks.

"It won't. Actually, it will allow your son to create a prompt of his own design," the principal replies.

I let the room fade around me, falling back into my own thoughts. No one had really challenged me to pursue the reservoirs of my imaginations. I mean, what kind of things can I come up with that hadn't been thought of already? Like talking robots, mythical races, and talking animals … where else is there to go? I rub my chin thoughtfully when once again I feel the pressure on my shoulder from my mother to my right.

"How long does he have?" my mom asks. Her hand lifts as I look up at her.

"As long as he needs, which hopefully won't be too long," the principal replies.

"Don't worry, Mom, I can do this," I add. My mom's familiar smile reappears when she looks down at me.

"I know you can," she replies, planting a kiss on the top of my head.

I look up as the principal shifts in his chair, the wheels groaning slightly. He gets to his feet, nearly as tall as my dad. He makes his way to the front of his desk.

"Well, I must be off. I have a meeting with the faculty," he says, extending his hand to my dad. They shake hands quickly, and then the principal makes his way to the door.

"Do you want this back?" my dad asks, holding up the report still in his hand.

The principal pauses, and turns his head. "Keep it," he says with a grin. "You should read it." He then turns the knob and the door opens wide, allowing him to step outside. Light floods the room as my parents walk around in front of me.

"Well, come on, honey, let's go home," my mom says.

I blow a tense breath between my lips as I stand, watching them make their way toward the door. The office aide waves farewell to my parents as they make their way to the door. I frown at her as I pass by, and she does the same, her distaste for me obvious.

My dad opens the door for my mom, and allows her through first. Once she steps into the hallway, he places his hand on my shoulder and stops me. I look up at him. "You gotta stop stressing us out," he says.

I nod and step into the hallway. I pause for a moment as I watch my parents pass through the glass doors, my mother smiling up at my dad. Suddenly, the bell for the end of the period rang as I stood in the middle of the hall. Doors swing open around me, kids erupting out. I watch as the hall fills with students who walk every which way, socializing, locker-emptying, and just simply walking to their next class. It borders on an uncontrollable chaos.

"See you soon," I mumble to myself.

I then begin to push through the shifting tides of fellow students. Finally, I find a gap large enough for me to make my way into traffic, allowing me to step into the flow. With a little pushing, I find myself moving forward until I reach the glass doors where my parents wait on the other side. I reach for the handle, but before I can take another step, a shadow grows on the pale floor beneath my shoes.

Turning back, I see Ralph. He says no words, just raises his hand into the air so his palm could face me. I look up at it and grin, delivering a mighty high five. It sends a jolt down my arm as I lower it back to my side. He nods his head in solidarity before stepping back into the flow.

I shake my hand against my pant leg as I turn back to see my parents holding the door open, giving me a look. I make my way outside, seeing my dad's black SUV at the curb, in between yellow buses. I pause as my parents climb into the car, feeling as if this should inspire me somehow; my release from the prison of school should flood me with ideas. The engine suddenly revs, and exhaust clouds up the clear air.

"You coming?" my mom calls.

I blink from my thoughts, smirking as I make my way down to the car. My dad unlocks the door as I pull the silver handle, sliding inside. Once my rear met the leathery texture, I shut the door behind me, looking out the window at the drab whiteness of the school as the car starts to move. Relief fills me as I watch the school get farther out of reach until it disappears, replaced by monotonous streets filled with cars.

I close my eyes, listening to the road noise as we drive home. Before long, we stop, and I open my eyes to see a pristine moment in time. Beyond the car next to us, an open field stretches into the distance, with park benches scattered around. However, what really caught my eyes is what's happening around the benches.

Several adults stand around with cameras and paint supplies. It's clear that they're just there on this sunny day to enjoy the blue sky. I wish I could be out there with them.

Suddenly, the red light turns green, and we once again begin to move along with the other vehicles. All I can see are streets filled with large buildings and people in colored suits as we found ourselves entering the land of business.

We pause at another red light, and I watch the light hanging in the breeze, undisturbed as cars pass beneath it. The surroundings become familiar as the light turns green and the large buildings fade to everyday houses. The brownish-green lawns in front of each one contrasts with the different shades of the structures. Each house is similar to the next, yet distinct in the tiniest details: a flag waving high, or the various cars sitting outside on the driveway. This is the suburban life I have always known.

The car slows as we near our house, gently turning before briefly rumbling up the driveway and toward a garage. I watch the garage door come closer in front of us as the car comes to a stop.

I look around for any signs of other kids as I reach for the door handle, before I remember my situation. My parents step out of the car, and make their way to the front door. I look down at the door, and open it as sunshine rains down onto the leathery surface of the door.

I step out onto the driveway, watching my parents disappear into the house. I make my way towards the single step which separates the doorway and the outside world. That single step splits everything; on one side, the air is clear, and the grass is green, meanwhile, inside the colors were variable and made worse by the artificial light around us.

I make my way inside the house, shutting the door behind me. My mom walks into the main room, switching on the light. The bulbs flicker on, pushing the darkness into the corners. I walk to the staircase, where faded wavy carpet leads the way to the next floor. Yet on that floor is the place that I call my sanctuary. My room, where I lay my head down at night, and also write things that the world would eventually see. I grin as I reach for the railing.

"Before you go running off to another world, make sure to wash your hands," my mom calls from the other room.

I look over to the kitchen, seeing her face peeking out from behind the door frame. She watches as I take another step upwards, nodding my acknowledgement. I then skip up the stairs.

In my mind, each step is a journey to a mysterious place. A place where, at the end, waits a world where I can create magic; magic that can cause inspiration for new characters, and even worlds beyond my own imagination. After I get to the final step, I pause, looking to the restroom which sits between me and my doorway.

Taking the necessary strides, I step onto the cold tile floor on the other side of the doorway. Once inside, I flick the light on, which allows me to see the mirror hanging above the sink. The porcelain is clean except for a couple of old drops of toothpaste. I turn on the faucet, causing water to splash into the basin. I reach my hands into the water, watching it swell over my skin as it crashes against my palm.

Before I waste anymore, I reach over for some soap, and squeeze some onto my hands. As the soap tries to run away, I slam my hands shut, sealing it inside. I then rub them together, causing bubbles to sprout between my fingers. The suds spread evenly all over my hands and wrists before I reach out for the handle and suddenly shut the water off.

I lift my hands to my forehead. I then slide them down to my chin, leaving a trail of suds across my face. Admiring my actions momentarily, I watch as the soap starts to drip off my chin. I then lower my face down into the sink to prevent anymore from falling onto the floor. Once more I turn on the water, and place my hands inside. The soap runs off, and spirals down into darkness. As the last bit of soap runs out of sight, I turn off the water, and reach for a single brown towel on a hook. I quickly turn to it, and place my hands on its linen surface.

After drying my hands thoroughly, I bring the towel toward my face. I dry off the water before I turn my attention to the open door. I flip the light switch off, hearing the faint sounds of the bulbs as they cool off.

Meanwhile, my focus remains on the single door to my left. It was the door which leads to everything I had ever known; the door which I thought of as more of a gateway. One to a thousand worlds besides this one. I approach slowly, feeling anticipation. My hand twists the door handle, and pushes against it. Behind the door, I find nothing out of the ordinary. My bed is still in one corner up against the wall as my desk sits across the way, and between them is a single dresser with various articles of clothing scattered on top.

Stepping inside, I close the door carefully behind me. I make my over to my desk, which my dad struggled to build a while back. I lean over, pulling out my laptop from one side. I place it onto the single flat surface between the pieces of particle board. It works perfectly because, after all, every writer starts somewhere. I flip up the cover, and admire my reflection in the blank screen. My finger then pushes down the power button, changing the dark screen into a variety of colors.

Suddenly, a generic image appears, and I press a random key on the keyboard. This sent the image away, and my desktop and a couple of important icons line up for me to use them. At the front is the word processor program which I had always used to place down my thoughts. Whether it was in poetic formation or in a full-length story, this program holds hours of my time.

I take a deep breath before double-clicking the mouse on top of the icon. It shoots up a window that fills up the screen over the blank wallpaper. The bar on top shows me how I am going to type, but never tells me what I was going to type. That was of my accord, an option

I thoroughly enjoy as my freedom of selection.

However, today is different because my hand has been dealt with a prompt of evolutionary art. I mean, how do you write something that hasn't been done? Can you really revolutionize art from just words on a keyboard? I stare blankly at the flashing black line as it waits for my thoughts to bubble up to the surface.

Finding nothing, I stare down at my fingers, which remain frozen above the letters, still as a stone. This must be what writer's block feels like, 'cause I had not even the faintest clue what to write. Not even a trace of an idea or an opening for one. My mind blanking on anything and everything, I let my hands retract to my side. My mind isn't one that I can just say to, "hey, focus on this given topic." I always let it be free to write whatever it wants and don't allow anyone to give me a prompt.

As I grunt in frustration, I push my chair back from the desk. I watch the white screen fade to darkness. The screensaver begins to take over, which allows me to think without the mockery of the blank page. I get up to my feet, and make my way over to the edge of my bed. I plop down onto the clumpy comforter which lays crooked on my bed. I dart my eyes around the room as I try to not think of the failed attempt before letting my eyes make their way back over to the dark screen. The screensaver flickers about as suddenly the sounds of the fan above my head catches my attention. I look upwards at the blades as they spin lazily, sending a gust down on me.

"What do I write about?" I grumble loudly.

"Anything your imagination can create," my dad's voice suddenly calls out from behind my bedroom door.

"Thanks, Dad," I said before I fell back onto my bed.

As my head settles onto the feathery surface, my brain continues to search for something to write about. Still nothing, just thoughts about my friends at school who were still there while I was here, coming up empty.

My eyes slowly close until finally, all I see is darkness. Time seems to slow around me as I lay there, and all I can sense is the air which lands on my skin. Before long, the dark shadows behind my eyelids flitter away and a bright light pierces the darkness. My eyes reopen to see the bright sun, which has sneaked out from between a pair of clouds.

I suddenly realize something isn't right and I struggle to take in where I am. When I look over my shoulder, I find the front door to my house. I realize I am outside as a bird calls nearby. I have no idea how I had gotten here, but nothing else seems out of reality. Before I can turn around, a horn echoes from all the way down the street. Next thing I know, the front door bursts open, and my parents are standing in the doorway. I watch as suddenly I, of all people, walk out from between them. A large white bus pulls up to the driveway, and I turn my attention back to myself as I stand with my arms at my side.

I'm surprised when I turn to look at me. A weight suddenly fills my hands and I look down to see a picture in my hands. It's smooth like glass, and I lift it up to block the scene before me. Suddenly, everything around me freezes, even the tree that had been blowing softly in the front yard.

Startled, I lose my grip on the picture, watching it fall to the ground. It shatters as it hits the sidewalk, causing the whole scene around me to shatter as well, plummeting me into darkness. I clench my eyes shut quickly, darkness consuming me.

I jump awake, realizing I'm still lying on my bed. A cold sweat drips down the back of my neck as the vivid thoughts fill my brain. I lift my hands to my face, wiping it dry. I don't have long to wonder about the dream as a knock suddenly echoes through the house. I look over to my bedroom door, trying to figure out where it is coming from as I slide off my bed. I walk over and cautiously open my door. Finding no one, I make my way through the doorway, turning to the railing before poking my head over it to see down by the front door. Another round of knocking echoes through the house as my dad makes his way over to the door. He presses his hands against the door before leaning to look through the peephole.

"Who is it?" my dad asks.

Another voice replies and I see my dad stand up straight before reaching for the door handle. He opens the door, revealing a man whose black dress shirt and pants contrast with his lighter complexion. He and my dad exchange a soft conversation until finally, my dad moves to the side. He looks up at the staircase catching sight of me. The man walks inside after taking off his hat, his dark brown eyes finding mine.

"Are you Walter?" he asks.

As I struggle to choose between a nod or actual words, my mom steps into my sight, buying me some time.

"That is my son, but the better question is, who are you?" my mom asks.

"I am sorry for the intrusion, but I am here to offer your son an invition to come to an art school," the man replies.

My interest starts to grow as I stare at the strange man.

"What kind of art school?" my mom asks, as if she knew what I would want to hear before any kind of decision.

"A school where students can develop their artistic visions, and create worlds beyond our imaginations," the man replies.

Before my mom can speak, he reaches inside of his jacket pocket and pulls out a brightly colored flyer which he gives to my mom. I watch as she opens it up, revealing various pages with writing inside of colorful boxes. Before I can see anymore, she shuts the papers and turns her attention up to me with a solemn look before looking back to the man.

"Will he be with other students?" my mom asks.

My eyes shifted to the man in time to see him nod his head.

"Yes ma'am," the man replies.

"What would he be learning there?" my mom asks.

"He will learn about various arts that will broaden his imagination," the man replies.

"Walter honey, please come downstairs and meet … " My mom looks at him, as if to ask his name.

"Vice Principal Mclemore," the man says, before adjusting his tie.

With a deep breath, I step around the curve of the railing make my way down as I keep my eyes on them. As I step off the last stair, I watch the vice principal extend his hand out to me. I look down to his hand before over to my mom, seeing her nod her approval, while my dad remains stern and mute to the side. A clammy feeling crept through my fingertips as I extend my hand towards him. His grip is firm as we shake hands.

"What school do you lead?" I ask him after swallowing thickly.

"He is from the School of Common Arts," my mom replies.

I look over to her to see her arms across her chest. Her eyes glitter with pride, even though I can tell she's trying to hide it.

"Yes, however," Vice Principal Mclemore says, drawing my attention, "Desean Dubois is the Head Principal of the school."

My mind races suddenly with a list of questions longer than a standardized test. I take a calming breath, and think of the first question that comes to mind. "What are Common Arts?"

"Photography, Drawing, Writing, and Music," he replies.

Obviously, I know where I fit into those subjects, but I honestly don't know much about any of the others. "So … why exactly have you come to see *me*?"

"To invite you to come to our school and strengthen your skills," the man replies, confirming what I thought he would say.

"I'm always open to new things that will grow my creativity," I say, looking over at my silent parents.

"So I guess that just leaves mom and dad, then," the man says, shifting his glance to them as well.

I look over to my dad as he walks around to stand next to my mom, who unfolds her arms. They both nod in approval, and suddenly all I can think about is what is this school?

I mean, really, what kind of school would actually want me? Yes, I am creative, and enjoy developing plots of my own choice, but I'm definitely not the most book-smart. Just as my thoughts return back to normal, I watch the vice principal as he makes his way outside. "I'll pick you up for your first day in the morning," he calls.

The First Day

The late morning sunlight blinds me as I step outside. I watch as a cloud sneaks its way in front of the sun, snuffing out the blinding light momentarily, revealing a quite familiar setting. The only difference is that today, behind my dad's car, is one of a compact size. Its shiny rims match the bright red paint job to perfection. I see Vice Principal Mclemore standing beside the car. He presses a remote, which causes the headlights to flash. I then watch as he walks over to the passenger door and opens it. As I continue to look on in silence, he looks back at me.

"It isn't a yellow school bus, but I hope it will do," he calls.

I turn back to look at my parents as they remain in the open doorway. "Are you sure?"

"We want you to be in a place that challenges your imagination to be the best it can be," my mom says.

I look back at the red car to find the open door and the vice principal sliding back into the driver's seat. My mind is filled with a thousand possibilities as I walk to the car. Vice Principal Mclemore starts the car as I slide inside. The leather interior looks similar to my parent's car, but the space is much smaller. I pause before pulling the door shut, seeing my parents walk over. My eyes start to well up as they both lean over, wrapping me in a massive hug. Once they step back, my dad shuts the door and a tear rolls down my cheek.

"Don't worry," the vice principal says to them through the window, "your son will be in great hands."

I look back when he shifts the car from out of park. The engine revs as the car moves backwards down our driveway.

My eyes never left my parents as they remain frozen in the driveway. I watch as they lift up their hands and wave farewell. I, too, raise my hand before the car moves up the street, causing me to lose sight of my parents. Once I can no longer see them, I shift my eyes in front of me. Then, just before the silence gets awkward, I spot the vice principal looking into the rear-view mirror.

"What are you looking at?" I ask.

"He is looking at me," another voice replies.

My head twists around when I realize that another person is sitting in the back seat of the car. A kid similar in age to myself, with black hair and hazel eyes, he has a pair of headphones around his neck and a laptop across his legs.

"How long have you been back there?" I ask in surprise.

"Since I picked him from up his school," the vice principal replies, keeping his eyes on the open road in front of us.

"My name is Roger O'Neil. What is yours?" Roger asks after pressing a button on the laptop.

"Walter Turner," I reply. I'm not sure how I missed him as he leans himself up against the door panel.

"Roger is a student with a unique perspective on the different aspects of music," Vice Principal Mclemore says when the car comes to a stop.

I look around to find myself in a part of a town emptier than the ones I have seen before. The trees outnumber the houses, and no one walks along the sides of the road. Even the stop signs that kept us in our place appear a tad bit rusty. Before I can take in any more of the surroundings, a whistle flows through my ears. Such a perfect blend of pitch and melody, it sends shivers down my spine. Looking back, my eyes catch sight of Roger placing a drive in front of his face. Once the whisper goes silent, he lowers the drive down into the computer. I watch as a red light flashes before turning solid. A couple clicks of the mouse later, and I begin to hear the whistling once again.

"How did you do that?" I ask. My eyes shift between his face and the laptop as the car starts to move once again.

"I have programmed this drive to record my sounds so I can edit it on my laptop," Roger replies.

I hear the mouse clicking and the buttons on the keyboard as Roger pushes them downwards. Once he pushes the final button, he looks down at the screen with a mixture of anxiety and glee. He sits back when an unusual sound begins to play. It was music, or at least that is what I fathomed it to be. My mind races as it tries to place the sound to the song, when suddenly the entire melody shifts completely. It is almost like there are two battling bands going against one another. Just before the drums can take over, they then drop off to slowly reveal his whistle. He then clicks once more before he looks into my watery eyes. I am speechless as my mind races, searching for the right word that I feel will do it justice. To my disbelief, this entire thing is all coming from the whisper I had heard moments earlier.

"That was amazing."

"Thanks," he replies.

Before our conversation can get any farther, I turn in my seat, realizing we're slowing down. My jaw drops, and my eyes swell as I spot the massive building sitting on top of the hill in front of us. It seems to extend to the horizon even though the drive up is merely a couple of seconds. As we came closer, the grass got greener, and the trees begin to look more in control. This couldn't be real. I mean, things seemed to be too perfect. I felt the silence as it lingered in the car before I hear Roger's laptop close.

"Welcome to school," the vice principal replies, pulling the car up to a set of winding stairs.

Roger and I sit silently for a moment, staring at the sight beyond the windows. It is strange though, 'cause there is not a single student outside.

"This is it?" Roger asks sarcastically.

I look over to see the lack of intrigue in his eyes as he reaches for the door. It pops open, which allows him to place his feet onto the gravel driveway. He extends to a full stretch before he shuts the door. I look down at my own door handle and squeeze it, which causes the door to open. The cold air seeps inside and causes goose bumps to roll over my arms. I step out of the car, and stand next to Roger, who starts to smile. Before he can speak, I shut the door and turn my attention back to the school. Suddenly, I feel the door shake as the window drops down inside of it.

"Welcome to the School of the Common Arts," Vice Principal Mclemore says.

The doors to the building swing open, revealing greenish lights that glow inside. Once more, the door shakes as the window rolls back into place. I feel the engine rev as the vice principal pulls away, leaving us alone. We watch the car as it pulls away, until it turns towards the other side of the building.

"I guess we should see what the big deal is," Roger says.

With a nod, we make our way inside. I had no idea what I expected to find inside, I just knew that I would regret it if my response was to back out now. Without a second thought, I step into the foyer, the pristine tiles laying before us and leading the way. We look all around until we both see the letters that make up Arts above us. Our attention then shifts down the hallway where lockers line the walls.

Yet, something didn't feel normal. I don't know if it is the windows that are built into the actual walls or the fact that everything is clean. I don't think I have ever been in a school that is this clean. The walls show no sign of age and the marble tiles are shining like they were just put in. Before we can go too far, a single person manifests, turning and walking in our direction. He is a tall man with a scruffy face. His hair is as white as the walls around us, matching his suit.

His skin contrasts with his white suit and in his hand he carries a wooden cane. I look over at Roger, who remains motionless, as the man stops before us. His eyes bounce between us as the wrinkles on his face tighten to show some youthfulness before he leans the cane against the doorway.

"How may I help you two?" the man asks, continuing to look at us.

I gulp to try to find an answer , glancing at Roger as he reaches into his pants pocket. From inside, he pulls out two cards. I quickly discover my name on the white one in black lettering. Meanwhile, on the other, I find Roger's name written in musical notes. He hands them over to the man who reaches out his wrinkly hand. He brings them closer to his face, examining them, and then looks back at us with a smile.

"I was told to give those to you," Roger says, breaking the silence.

The man turns his attention to him before looking back down at the cards. "By whom?"

"Vice Principal Mclemore," I reply.

"Well then, so which one of these belong to you?" the man asks as he reaches out the two cards.

Both Roger and I look down at the two cards. He reaches down first and grabs hold of the card with his name on it. The man then turns towards me as I reach down for my card. I then place it into my own pocket.

"Okay, so you are Roger, and you are Walter?" he asks.

"We are," Roger and I reply.

"And who are you?" Roger asks.

"I am the principal of this school," the man replies.

"Desean Dubois?" I ask, remembering the vice principal speaking his name to my parents and me.

"Yes, but you can call me Principal Desean," he replies.

Roger looks over at me before he turns back to Principal Desean. We watch as he looks downwards at a brown watch around his wrist. After a moment, Desean lifts his head to look over his shoulder. Down from the depths of the hallway, a short shadow slides into the wall with a thump. We watch as a boy, about our age and with his hair parting to the direction of his feet, leaving his eyes hidden behind wire frames, shakes his head before continuing to run down the hall. A camera hangs around his neck with some weird mechanical thing protruding from it. It is something I have never seen before. More importantly though, behind the camera's strap, is a bright green lanyard. At the end of it is a green card with black lettering that spells 'photography', which I catch briefly before it hides once more behind the camera. He turns his eyes to the principal, who just shakes his head.

"Sorry I'm late, but I saw a beautiful thing which required a picture," the boy says quickly. He seems worried for a moment before the expression on the principal's face changes to a grin.

"Show it to me," Desean replies.

The boy lifts the camera, moving his finger to the left a couple times, and then pressing something on the back. We watch the machine behind it turn on and a picture prints out of it. He lifts it from the printer, and then hands it to the principal, who frowns in confusion.

"What's wrong?" the student asks, watching the principal study the picture.

"This is just a flower," Desean replies before flipping it, which reveals it to us.

The image is, in my opinion, pretty good. It is a bright yellow flower surrounded on all sides by greenery. I mean nothing unusual, but very nice.

"I think it's a pretty good picture," I say as I look over at Roger, who shrugs.

"It gets better," the student replies.

He walks over, pinching the picture in his fingers. It distorts momentarily before returning to normal as he lets go of it. Roger and I watch as the picture suddenly begins to move. On its own, time in the frames passes, which causes the images to change. An orange and black monarch butterfly flutters into the frame, landing on the flower, its wings settling along the leaf's surface. Before we can see any more, it stops, freezing the image of the butterfly on it.

Desean turns it back over in order to see the new image waiting for him on the picture. We watch as his face starts to glow with excitement.

"Now that is a magical piece," Desean says.

I quickly step closer to Roger, and lean towards him as he remains focused on the two in front of us. "Did you just see that?" I watch him nod his head when suddenly Desean turns his eyes back to us.

"Pardon the switch of subjects, but Jordan here is going to show you to your classes," Desean says. "I must be off. Enjoy your time here." He then steps back into the hall disappearing from view.

Jordan looks at both of us. "Say Cheese," he says suddenly.

Before either of us can prepare ourselves, Jordan snaps a picture. The bright flash blinds us for a moment as Jordan looks down at his printer. Once more, the printer turns green, except this time nothing prints out. The green light turns red as a look of concern appears on his face.

"Everything okay?" I ask.

Then it all goes dark.

Back to the Theater

I turn to Periwinkle, seeing him clapping his hands gently as suddenly the theatre around us rumbles before returning to a stand still.

"What was that?" I ask, looking around at the falling lines of dust.

"The end of that picture," Periwinkle replies. He grabs hold of the remote once again and presses the arrow key, which pulls up another screen. On it, three images appear, revealing a series of names. The first one that we just watched, I'm assuming, is *The Council.* He then shifts the outline to another icon with the title *Element.*

"What is the story behind that one?" I ask.

"Element vs element, allies vs enemy," Periwinkle replies.

"No offense, but it sounds pretty generic," I say, watching Periwinkle's face sour.

"True, however, each idea is unique per mind," Periwinkle replies, once more reaching for the remote.

"One last thing," I say, causing him to look back to me.

"Ask away," Periwinkle replies.

"More popcorn please," I say, pointing my hand down to the nearly-empty bag between us.

With a shake of his head, Periwinkle lifts his hand and snaps his fingers, causing the room to vibrate with the sound. Then, before my eyes, the bag shakes until kernel after kernel appears. Once the bag is about to overflow, the kernels quit falling. Levels sufficient, I turn my attention back to the bare screen as Periwinkle lifts up the remote control once more.

"Lost story number two … The Elements," Periwinkle says deeply. The screen twists and turns until it finally reveals an image quite similar to the one previous. Shades of brown overtake the landscape with signs of life sparce throughout the screen. "Narrator talk time."

The Elements

In the year 3000, a lot has changed since the time of human rule. Sorcerers have taken control of society. From the vacant landscape in the once fruitful countryside, to the now barren capitals, society has been turned upside down. This story takes us to the area known now as Morza, a once fruitful and prosperous location. The once prominent skyscrapers that decorated the horizon have been burned and the air is so thick that just taking a breath is an unfortunate task. Now the question remains, where are the guides to a brighter day and when are they coming?

As the sun begins to labor through the sky, Desmond's eyes open to a pale living room and he quickly wipes his eyes. Then with a mighty yawn, he sits up on a dusty sofa, looking around for any sign of change. To his disappointment there is nothing, and Desmond shakes his head and gets up from the sofa, his feet landing on pale gray carpeting. After stretching for a moment, he turns his attention to the far wall where a lumpy blanket is covering a thin mattress.

"Come on Marion, it's time to rise and shine," Desmond says as he watches as the lump turns over, releasing a painful moan.

After a couple of seconds, the blanket remains still as Desmond looks on from the center of the floor. He shakes his head and lifts his hand, a gust of wind erupting from the ground and lifting the blanket into the air. The gust reveals the body of teenager, not much younger than Desmond, beginning to flop around the damp air. Marion tries to reach out and grab the blanket, only to have Desmond lift the blanket beyond his fingertips.

"Fine, I'll get up," Marion replies, rolling from the springy mattress.

Satisfied, Desmond turns around and goes underneath the broken doorframe to the bathroom, closing the curtain separating the two rooms. He heads to the cracked sink and turns the rusted faucet, water slowly streaming into the dusty bowl. Desmond then reaches out his hands into the bowl, allowing the water to run over them.

Looking up into the mirror fragments, he sees a reminder of the damage life has done to his young skin, graying hairs on his head to the scars and bruises dotting his face. He closes his eyes as he quickly splashes some of the water against his face. As the water drips from his chin, he struggles to think of positive things in life. However, before he can get too deep into thought, a sudden a pounding on the front door sends chills down his spine. He quickly shuts off the water and yanks the curtain back, standing in the living room where his brother is.

"Open up the door or we shall send it flying!" a voice yells from the other side as another round of pounding shakes the door.

After taking a deep breath, Desmond quickly reaches out and opens the door to reveal the two men on the other side. "Controllers, how may I help you today?"

"We have come on behalf of the High Sorcerer," one of the men says.

"I am Desmond Jones. How may I be of service?" he asks with a touch of sarcasm.

The guard turns to his fellow officer, before sucker-punching Desmond to the ground. Before his brother can move a muscle, the other guard begins to glow and three clones appear from nowhere. Two of them charge Desmond, and grab hold of each of his arms, while the third clone backs Marion into a corner. The Controllers move towards Desmond.

"Don't hurt him!" Marion yells as he watches the Controllers stand motionless while the clones pick Desmond up off the floor.

Still woozy, Desmond's eyes flicker as one of the Controllers turns to the other and nods his head. Before the brothers' very eyes, the Controller manifests a large black box in his hands. He turns, and the lid opens, revealing an object with a bluish glow. He reaches in and pulls out a mask, which appears to have tubing going from the main part to the back.

"What are you going to do to him?" Marion demands, trying to find a way past the clone.

The Controller remains silent as he lifts the mask in his hands before turning back to face the groggy Desmond. "Now he can join his brothers on the outside lands," the Controller says with a half smirk as he begins to attempt to place the mask on Desmond.

Marion suddenly tries to get past the clone only to be slammed back into the corner. The vibrations bring Desmond back to himself, and he flails his arms up and down as the clones struggle to hold him still. As his anger grows, his eyes turn pale white and a sudden heaviness encompasses the room.

The Controllers stop in their tracks, their movements slowed by the heaviness wrapping around their limbs. Suddenly, the clone on Desmond's left side crashes through the floor as everyone looks on. Then, before the Controllers can react, the clone to his right lifts off the ground and begins to float uncontrollably before crashing through the wall next to Marion. The Controller drops the mask onto the splintering floor in disbelief as Desmond rises to his feet.

"Stand down, sorcerers!" Desmond roars as he watches the other clone de-materialize, leaving just the two original Controllers.

"We shall for now, but you will put that mask on. Otherwise, the real titans of sorcery will punish you," one says before disappearing into thin air. As the calmness slowly returns to the room, Marion looks at his brother as he stares at the mask sitting on the ground.

"Brother, everything okay?" Marion asks, walking toward Desmond as he reaches for the mask.

Without a reply, Desmond grabs a tight hold of the mask and lifts it up as he moves to his feet. "What has become of the heroes of humanity?" Desmond asks, snarling as his hands tighten around the mask.

As Marion watches in confusion, Desmond's eyes gloss over and he sends the mask flying through the wall. "Humanity was never a match for sorcery in anything I have ever read," Marion replies as

Desmond turns around to face him.

"Brother, this is no book in a library. This is reality," Desmond says as he walks up to his brother and places his hand on his shoulder.

Marion nods his head at his brother, who takes a deep breath to help calm himself down.

"I must go to work brother, since you are in no shape," Marion says as he takes a step back and heads over to the makeshift rack by the door. On the rack hangs a dirty coat and a mask that Marion's friend, Dimitri, had let him borrow.

Desmond, feeling the air leave his lungs, watches his brother put the coat over his shoulder as he grabs the mask off the wall. For a brief second, Marion pauses to stare at the mask as he does every day, knowing the pain it is about to cause him. He then turns it around and slowly moves it towards his mouth as tears begin to slip from his eyes in anticipation. Once the mask is firmly on his face, it suddenly begins to sear his skin as it takes hold of his mouth and nose.

Desmond can do nothing but watch as the mask secures to his brother's face, leaving him with tears pouring off his cheeks. Once the fusion is complete, Marion drops to his knees as he struggles to point at the pocket in the coat. Desmond quickly rushes over and opens the flap, pulling out a vial filled with a glowing blue liquid. He quickly pops open the cap as the color starts to leave his brother's face, removing the cap on the mask and pouring every drop of the liquid directly into the mask. Once the vial is empty, all the color returns to Marion's face as he regains his strength.

"Are you okay?" Desmond asks as his brother quickly wipes away the last few tears on his face.

With a small nod, Marion opens the rusty door and steps out into the hall as his brother remains behind. After looking back for a moment, Marion quickly closes the door behind him, leaving Desmond in silence.

Now alone, Desmond quickly debates his next move before suddenly running after his brother. He quickly runs to the door and steps outside, only to find no one in the hallway. He looks up, spotting a figure stepping into the chalky, dust-filled air. He quickly runs toward the swirling outside air, only to feel the oxygen being sucked from his lungs with each step.

Without even realizing how far he's gone, Desmond finds himself in the middle of the emptiness in the outside world. Unable to breathe, Desmond stumbles his way back into the safety of the hall, feeling the air returning to his lungs. As he contemplates the next move, the sandy wind suddenly stops in mid-air, and drops to the ground. His breaths slow and he turns his sight to the clear air, where shadows begin to appear. Desmond watches as a squad of guards holding staffs of various glows form in front of a crowd of people.

As the crowd gets closer, the fully-armored legion of sorcerer guards walk straight past the open hallway, plainly dressed people just like his brother following in tow, all of them wearing the very mask that Marion had on his face before he took off. Once the final row of people marches out of the ruins of town, the back patrol of sorcerers stop, a building shy from where Desmond stands.

"They shall do finely," one of the patrol members says to the guard next to him.

Desmond watches as they slam their staffs onto the broken street and begin to levitate upwards, returning to the rear of the march. They circle the crowd as they get farther away from the town center with each passing breathe. Worried about his brother, he scans the rest of the area, suddenly spotting four bodies lying amongst the dirt and broken stones. The worst imaginable thoughts start to flow through his head and, without a second thought, he explodes out of the hallway and out into the street.

He quickly kneels next to the first body and with all his might he manages to rip the mask off its face. To his relief, the face underneath was not his brother's, which provides him a moment of relief, despite the other bodies. He quickly drops the mask onto the ground as he turns his attention to the next body. As he stands to the side of it, all he can imagine are the different scenarios as he slowly kneels. Just as he reaches for the mask, Desmond gets a chill in his bones.

"Excuse me, peasant. What are you doing out on the street?" a voice demands from behind Desmond as a single tear begins to roll down his cheek.

Desmond rises to his feet in silence and turns around to find three guards in front of him.

"You better answer when the leader asks you a question. Or would you prefer a meeting with Kresto?" one of the guards snaps.

Desmond remains silent as his eyes meet the cold gaze of the three guards. He watches as their hands tighten around their weapons. "My apologies, I was merely here looking for my brother."

The three guards turn to one another, as if to leave him, when suddenly the one in the center shoves Desmond to the ground with an explosion of power from his hands. Desmond slides across the ground from the force of the magic, struggling to get back to his feet. The guards laugh at the pain on his face.

"Know your place as a powerless human and go home," the guard says as he points his wooden staff in the distance.

Desmond stands silent and motionless in front of them, closing his eyes and trying to keep his cool.

"Do you not hear anymore?" one of the guards demands, stepping toward Desmond. "Here let me help!" He suddenly fires another pulse of magic at Desmond.

This time, Desmond opens his blue eyes and quickly smacks the pulse from the air, sending it plowing into the ground. The guards are shocked as Desmond steps forward menacingly. Before Desmond can take another step, all three of the guards fire a pulse in his direction.

Before they can reach him, Desmond shoots out his hands and sends out a wave of magic that rocks the sandy ground, launching it at the guards. The sand and rocks start to pelt and scratch the guards, who shield their eyes from the onslaught. After staggering around blindly for a moment, Desmond appears inches from the captain. Once more, his eyes begin to glow and the earth under their feet quake, causing them to look down. Before they can react, vines suddenly shoot from the ground, grabbing hold of Desmond's feet and hands as the quaking ceases. The vines quickly yank Desmond to the ground, pinning him there as he struggles to break free.

"Oh, great. The Gang of Earth is here," one of the guards mutters as the ground begins to rumble around them.

They watch as three waves of sand and earth crash downward, each forming a humanly shape. They form into solid bodies, eyes and mouths and hair appearing. Smiles appear on their faces, to the dismay of the three guards.

Meanwhile, Desmond remain motionless on the ground.

"Wow, not even a thank you, Lindsay?" one says, continuing to stretch out his joints to their correct shape.

"I know, right. How rude. But hey, can you blame them when they got bested by a human?" Lindsay replies, looking down at Desmond.

"He is no ordinary, didn't you see that?" one of the guards yells as he points over to the mound of dirt from the wave that Desmond had sent against them.

"You want us to believe you based on a dirt mound?" the commander of the Gang of Earth replies as he turns to Lindsay and the other guard with a huge smile. They begin to laugh hysterically as the guards begin to shake in anger.

As the groups continue to bicker, Desmond grabs hold of the stems around his wrists and watches as smoke curls from them. After a couple of seconds, tiny flames erupt just long enough for him to break his hands loose.

"Seriously, didn't we wipe out any signs of rogue activity?" Lindsay asks as the rest look over to her.

"I thought so," one of the guards replies as he pokes Desmond in the back with his staff.

"Well then, let's see this thing," the commander of the Gang of Earth says as Lindsay spins her hand, causing the vines around Desmond's feet to lift him into the air. Before he is completely upside down, Desmond manages to scrape handfuls of dirt into both hands. The six guards look on as Lindsay takes a couple of steps forward.

However, before she can say a word, Desmond quickly lifts his torso and throws the dirt towards the sky. As the guards watch the dirt fall harmlessly, Desmond attempts to free his ankles from the vine trap. The guards then turn their attention back to Desmond as the dust settles.

"Was that what you call magic?" the commander laughs as Desmond stares at his hands in wonder.

Desmond looks back up into the guard's eyes. "No, this is magic," Desmond says, snapping his fingers, causing a giant wall of earth and sand to surround him.

The guards quickly begin to try to break through the wall, while inside, Desmond melds through the vines around his feet. Once free, Desmond aims his hands downward, diving down through the swirling sand underneath him. Just as the ground swallows him up, the wall crumbles down, not a single grain out of place as the guards stare in shock.

Back at Desmond's house, sand rains down from the roof and onto the floor. After a second, Desmond crashes through the ceiling, landing hard on the mound of sand covering the ground. Struggling to regain his breath, he slowly lifts himself up to his feet as he brushes off the sand.

"That was a close one," Desmond whispers, looking around the barren room.

He makes his way over to the window and looks outside to find some of the guards kicking around at the sand while the others stand back from the mound. With a chuckle, he steps back from the window, just as a knock at the door garners his attention. His head turns, wondering who could be at his door, slowly making his way over. A second round of knocking occurs as Desmond reaches for the doorknob. He turns the doorknob and opens the door, surprised to find nothing but open air on the other side. Confused, Desmond shuts the door, but as he turns around, a third round of knocking fills the room. He quickly opens the door to once again find nothing but emptiness on the other side.

"Looking for something?" a mysterious voice suddenly asks.

Desmond spins around, searching for the source of the voice. "Who's there?" he demands, searching the room carefully. He jumps when suddenly one of the pillows on the sofa flies across the room into a wall.

"I guess I can't blame you for not seeing something so small in comparison," the voice replies as Desmond continues to look for the source.

"Where are you?" Desmond asks, continuing his search.

"On the top of the sofa," the voice replies.

Desmond looks over to the sofa, spotting a green lizard in between the crevices in the fabric.

"Good afternoon, Desmond," it says with a lizardly smile.

"This can't be—there is no such thing as a talking lizard," Desmond says quickly.

"This coming from the guy who made it rain sand inside of his own living room," the lizard responds.

"Indeed, this is true, but a talking lizard does come across a bit far-fetched," Desmond says.

"Let me help you then," the lizard says as it leaps behind the sofa.

Before Desmond can speak a word, a white light begins to irradiate from behind the sofa and a shadow arises on the wall behind it. As quick as the light appears, it then vanishes, and a man with graying hair appears behind the sofa.

"This any better?" asks the man.

"Yes, it is. Who you are?" Desmond responds as the man steps quietly around the sofa and then sits down upon it.

"My name is Jacoby," says the man as he stretches out his arms while Desmond watches him.

"And, what exactly are you doing here in my home?" Desmond asks as Jacoby looks back at him.

"I'm here to teach you," replies Jacoby.

"Teach me what?" Desmond asks.

"The way to control your power so you may achieve all that you may desire," says Jacoby as a flame ignites from his palm.

Suddenly, the flame freezes, along with the other images on the screen. Bit by bit, the image fades and returns to black, forcing Periwinkle to once again place the remote down onto the console between chairs.

Interruption

Before we can speak, both of us spot a shadow different from either of ours. We both look back, finding Edalpo perched on a groove on the back wall beneath the projector.

"When did you get here?" I ask.

Edalpo tilts his head before shifting his gaze upon me. "Sometime during the first act," he caws.

The room begins to rumble violently suddenly, causing the tiles on the roof to quiver. Just as I brace my hands on the sides of the chair, the room stabilizes, allowing the three of us to settle back into our places. Our breaths return as the seconds pass without more shaking.

"I heard nothing," I whisper to Periwinkle.

"Me neither," Periwinkle says softly.

Together, we turn our heads to see Edalpo reaching deep within the feathers of his wings. He then lifts his beak back and look over at us, relaxing his wings to his sides. We turn back to the screen as Periwinkle lifts the remote back into the air. As his finger drops toward the play button for the final picture, suddenly a loud screech echoes through the room. He looks over at me just as I look over at him.

"How about we try a different dimension for this final picture?" Edalpo asks, causing us to turn our gazes to him.

"What do you mean?" Periwinkle asks.

Sitting in silence, I watch as Edalpo reaches his beak within the shadows and then pulls out three pairs of glasses. With a swift flick, both Periwinkle and I grab hold of a pair each as Edalpo keeps the other.

I look down at the glasses, which have a red lens on one side and a blue lens on the other, before turning my gaze to Periwinkle, watching as he places the glasses on his nose over his eyes. I then look to Edalpo, who places the glasses above his beak. Finally, I place the glasses over my eyes, watching the lenses change my vision, the two colors blending into one dimensional space and turning the grayish walls into a vibrant mix of blue and red. It is a strange sight, but I seem to be the only one surprised. I am freaking out inside, especially when I looked down at the floor as it sways back and forth, like waves over my feet.

"What is going on here?"

"This is how you are going to watch the third film," Periwinkle replies.

Suddenly, the walls slam to the ground, revealing rows and rows of books with an occasional table between them. The image zips forward, all the way toward a main room with two glass doors in front of us. Next to the doors, a large office desk sits in front of an open doorway and the image stops just above the top of the counter. Beyond the stacks of books, a librarian dressed in a suit sits, eating waffles as globs of syrup drop to the plate below.

He pauses with his bite of waffle just shy of his mouth before he lets go of the fork, sending it crashing to the puddle of stickiness. He turns sternly to the half-eaten chunk of waffle, deeply exhaling in exasperation. His palms plant themselves with a thud, launching the librarian to a stand as the chair goes sliding out of view. He shifts his weight in our direction before taking large steps which vibrate through the floorboards toward us.

"How can I help you?" the librarian asks, making it to the counter. Among his open hands, books of various sizes and colors attempt to distract us from the thin layer of dust between them.

"I'm looking for the Elements."

The librarian's face changes from disgust to intrigue as the title left my lips. He lifts his hand up to his salt and pepper goatee, rubbing it gently before turning his attention to the various bays at the other end. I watch his eyes shift over each one before he turns his attention back to me. Before he can speak, a bell rings out causing both of us to look to the front of the room.

We discover the front door being held open by a teenager, fair in complexion, his clothing pressed and a bright red bowtie across his neck. His pants match with his jacket, and his formal shoes are a leathery material. Double-bowed white laces cross the black shoes, and a set of brown socks peeked out from under his pants. My eyes make their way up toward his brown eyes, which sit below an all-black top hat like the one Periwinkle wears.

"How can I help you?" the librarian asks.

The young man gulps down some saliva before his face goes as white as the laces on his feet. "Sir Gustavo, the Pancakeries have opened up another base just doors from this library."

Just as he finishes speaking, three brown, circular objects smack against the glass of the door before dripping down to the ground. The young man's eyes shift to the golden trail left behind as he screams in fear. Before either of us can say a word, he bolts from the doorway and down the cobblestone sidewalk, out of view.

I then turn to the librarian, who has crumpled up his hands into fists, the veins swelling beneath the skin in his wrists. "Were those things pancakes?"

"Vile things indeed," the librarian replies, turning his gaze back to the rows of book as he calms. Continuing to examine the bays, his eyes stop, and a smile grows on his face. He lifts his hand up and shoots out his index finger into the direction of a set of bays under a flickering light. "Element is over there."

"Why are they so far away from the others?" I ask.

"With every completed idea sits a dozen unfinished titles," Gustav answers.

"I still don't get it," I reply.

"That is the Unfinished section," Gustav replies, shifting my attention to the bay once again.

Hesitantly, I step away from him and make my way over to the flickering section of the library. With each passing step, I feel something pulling me into its direction. I dodge the line of leather couches in the middle of the room, finding myself steps away from the line of light before it flickers into darkness. I look up to see myself between two bays, bland carpet splitting them down the center. Above me, a sign hangs down from rusty chains which creek with a passing breeze from the nearby air vent.

I make out the word 'fiction' before the light has a chance to flicker off, and I make my way down the rows of books. Each cover is empty as far as the eye can see, and I start to wonder how I'm supposed to find the one I am looking for. Then, before my eyes in the center of the row, two books in solid colors stand out from the rest. Not only are they untouched by dust, but the binder has writing inside. The one on the right read *Elements*, while the one on the left contained the word *Murdio*.

"Grab the one on the left," a chorus of voices echo around me.

Slowly, I feel myself reaching out for it, away from the final picture. Unable to break the mysterious force guiding my hand toward it, I watch as I grab hold of *Murdio*. I then pull it out of the line of books and bring it closer to my body. My eyes dart downward at the orangish cover with a single cursive word written at the top of the page.

After reading the word *Murdio*, I shift my gaze over the remainder of the cover, which is a mixture of oranges and blacks and other shades sprinkled throughout. In the center of the page, an angelic body kneels with a pair of wings darting upwards from its muscular back. At its feet, the remains of a halo are spread along the ground, keeping the angel's aura in place. As my eyes drift downwards, a glimmering light streaks from top to bottom across the cover, forcing me to look over my shoulder. In shock, I step back as I catch sight of a beaming light dropping from the cracking tiles in the roof toward the carpet below.

"This no longer belongs amongst the others," a single voice murmurs.

Palm side up, a skeletal hand appears through the light, extending out to me. Looking down upon the fleshy bones as they remain rigid in thin air, I hesitantly move the book toward it. Just as I place the book within the fingers, they retract, entrapping it inside. My hand barely escapes its grasp as I watch the hand remain just on the outskirts of the light. As I release a breath, the hand pulls back and disappears, the light disappearing along with it.

I look down at my hand and then back to the row of books, unsure of what I just witnessed. As confirmation, I find the empty spot alongside *Elements*, which was my initial purpose.

"Thank you," the voice speaks before drifting out among the buzzing of the flickering light above.

Once more, I stand alone with no body to match the voice, so I return my gaze to the single book in front of me. Not waiting for another command, I reach my hand out toward the spine of the book.

"My apologies, sir," the librarian suddenly calls through an intercom system.

"For what?" I call back, keeping my eyes on my hand, frozen inches from the book.

"I should have warned you about books moving from incomplete to complete," he says. "That should be all for today, so you shouldn't have any more intrusions."

"Hope you're right," I whisper as I wrap my hand around the book. Once I get a firm grasp, I slide the book from out of its spot and bring it closer to me. I turn the book over to the front side to reveal the half-torn cover. All that remains is the first three letters and a towering wave of water.

Before I can open it, the book starts to pulse, sending vibrations down my arms. Traveling toward my shoulders, the numbness fades just before reaching them and suddenly I feel something at my feet. My eyes shift downward, just in time to watch the entire carpet sink beneath an ankle- deep layer of water. The water, bluish-green in color, stops rising just shy of the bottom of the first shelf of books.

Picking my foot up and sending water tumbling down to the puddles, I watch as the books remain dry. Suddenly, the flickering light above burns out, throwing the ends of the bay into darkness. Looking left then right, I find myself in a murky glow as the water begins to gather itself to one end. My eyes follow the retreating water, when suddenly pounding thunder fills the room. My heart jumps and I helplessly listen as the sounds cease, giving way to ripples within the carpet. A tidal wave suddenly bolts out of the darkness, heading in my direction.

I turn to run away through the puddles of water remaining as the wave continues to bear down upon me. Feeling like I won't make it, I catch a glimpse of the end of the bay. Before I can turn the corner, I catch a reflection of the approaching wave as drops of water crash down upon my back. Then, just before it can slam into the ground, I roll out of the way, avoiding the falling water. Struggling to recover, I look over at the bay to see nothing out of the ordinary. Not a puddle, not even a drop, just the usual rows of books beneath the flickering light. Unable to comprehend what I'd just experienced, my jaws drop in shock and I look back down at the dry ground. I make my way to my feet, looking at the books once again.

"You break it you buy it," the librarian's voice suddenly rings out above my head.

"Got it," I whisper, wiping the dust from my pant legs.

Exhaling, my breath slows as I spot something in my hand. To my disbelief, *Elements* is still in my possession. Except, something is different about the cover.

Gone is the drawing of the wave and in its place is a blazing inferno. Unable to digest the change, my nostrils flare as the smell of smoke and cinders fills my nose. I cautiously look over as an orange glow appears from the next bay over. The sounds of crackling takes over, and my eyes swell with water from the smoke as I catch sight of the blazing inferno happening between the sections of books. Unable to move, a warmth fills my hands, causing me to look down.

The book feels like it's on fire and I drop it quickly, allowing the pain to dissipate. The redness in my hands fades and I watch the orange glow between the bookshelves fade away, along with the accompanying crackling of fire. Kneeling, I reach for the book which, to my surprise, has undergone a cover change once again. It has grown, adding another column next to the towering wave and swirling chain of flames. I glance over to the bookshelf, finding it unscathed from the flames. Once more, the light in the library darkens, and the sound of thunder rattles the tiles overhead. My eyes drift upward to see a line of clouds covering the entire roof.

Lightning flashes around the roof and a sudden breeze starts to push against me. It picks up speed, pushing me toward the next set of shelves beyond where I stand. Taking a of couple steps, the pressure rises on my entire body, and I struggle to grasp one of the massive shelves to keep myself in place. I peek around the corner, surprised to see pockets of swirling wind. Leaves flurry through spinning funnels, rising and spinning about before falling helplessly back to the floor. I watch as the leaves merge back into the carpet as the spiraling winds calm down. However, once the final funnel dissipates, a new trembling noise echoes throughout the library.

From out of the swelling clouds above, a funnel drops down and starts to spin angrily, sucking in the books on the shelf. Flung from the funnel, the books land back in their spots on the shelf, their pages ruffling from the wind. I struggle to on as lightning bolts crash down to the carpet. With each strike, dark spots appear on the carpet and the tornado starts to unravel.

Section by section, it swirls uncontrollably as the clouds above calm. The lightning fades, causing the winds to drop to a soft breeze that ruffles the books. Finally, the wind disappears, returning the aisle back to normal. Seeing not a page out of place nor tear upon the covers, I look down at the book in my grasp, seeing a third column on the title page with the image of a tornado.

My eyes shift over to the remaining column missing from the cover, wondering what comes next. First was water, then fire, then wind … I don't like the idea of what comes next. Before I can give it much thought, a noise rings out from overhead.

"Hope you are still in one piece!" a voice screeches from the speaker.

I shake my head in disbelief, suddenly seeing the shelves disappear into darkness. I take a step forward warily, when something lands upon my feet. I look down, seeing a speck of a dirt and a tiny pebble made their way on top of my toes. I frown, and then another mound of dirt spills from out of the darkness.

As the mound grows, I step back, causing the dirt to shift onto the library carpet. I look down at the book then, bringing the it closer to stare once more upon its smearing verbiage. I then shift my eyes back to the wall of darkness, thinking about what stands behind its shield. With a bit of hesitation, I lunge forward, the space around me falling into the shadows.

A bright light suddenly appears overhead and its glow brightens the land around me. My eyes shift down to find the book gone and a sandy land beneath my shoes. Between the grains of sand, chunks of rock stand, waiting for a single breeze to roll them along. Then, from out of the calm, an explosion mushrooms into the sky, with another following behind. Before long, a shadow appears on the horizon, clouds of sand threatening to engulf it.

Suddenly, goosebumps dot my arms and a chill creeps up my back as I realize I'm watching a man running from something. As he runs toward me, I get a closer look at him.

His face is torn by a lifetime of battles and his hair is filthy with sand. He struggles to keep his nostrils free of debris with a torn handkerchief. His clothes are torn from the rough sand, and he turns his hands up, causing the ground next to me twist and spin. Soon, the sand drops away into a single, dark hole and the man jumps high into the hot air, suddenly falling down into the center of the hole.

Just as he disappears, the creatures aboard the mounts made of earth appear over the horizon, unleashing another round of blasts in my direction. My breath quickens as my mind fills with panic. I'm unable to move, and I watch the blast get closer until, just before it hits me, it stops. Just like that—dead in its tracks—it remains still as a stone, along with the rest of the scene. Everything, from the clouds above to the dissipating swirl at my side, pauses and disappears before my eyes. The silence and darkness overtake everything, allowing my heartbeat to drum through the hollow space. Suddenly, a clap rings out and the light to returns. I find myself back within the confines of the library.

Struggling to process the events, I rub my fingers against something in the palm of my hand. Looking down, I find the book, its cover finally complete. Now, the word *Elements* is in gold letters with all four pillars beneath it.

As I attempt to turn the cover to see what lies beneath, the lights inside the library fade away. Inside the darkness, my eyes shift all around for even a particle of light when a spotlight turns on from above. It reveals a single wooden desk just steps from me, allowing me to walk toward it. Cautiously, I make my way over and see a single red button with two lines in the middle. Above it, the word 'Press' is painted on in black lettering. I then look over at the book in my right hand, placing it slowly on the desk. Once it was out of my hands, I push down on the button, which turns off the spotlight, sending the entire library into total darkness.

Back from the Library

Before long, the image splits into red and blue sections, which shift upwards, revealing the faces of Periwinkle and Edalpo staring back at me.

"Welcome back," they say together.

Unable to speak, my eyes water as they dart about, taking in the theatre surroundings. My feet fall back down to the ground and a crunch echoes through the room. I lean forward to discover a blanket of kernels covering the floor. I look up at Periwinkle and Edalpo, who keep their eyes upon me. "Everything okay?"

"You tell us," Edalpo chirps, turning his attention to Periwinkle.

"You turned white as a ghost, so we decided to cut off the movie," Periwinkle says, causing my attention to shift to him.

"You would have too, looking at a blast of magical energy," I reply.

"Yea, Guillermo does have a powerful imagination," Periwinkle says, smirking before turning to Edalpo.

"Do you think he is ready?" Edalpo asks, turning his head.

My eyes shift to Periwinkle, who lifts one of his hands into the air. His fingers curl inwards, allowing his thumb to remain sticking outward, in a thumbs-up position. Edalpo grins before fluttering upwards to allow Periwinkle to return to his chair. A harness then appears above both of our heads, dropping down around our bodies. They lock into place on the legs of the chair and suddenly the large screen in front of us lifts, leaving a hole in its place. Meanwhile, the floor between us splits in the center, allowing a track to lift upwards. Once secure, the chairs jolt forward onto the tracks, gaining speed as they approach an opening.

"Watch out for the big drop!" Edalpo chirps.

"Where are we going?" I ask, causing Periwinkle to turn to me.

"The next ring," Periwinkle replies as the chairs gather speed.

"What is the next ring?" I ask, bracing myself as the chairs come to a stop. The chairs hang at the edge of the dim lights, gaping darkness awaiting us.

"Creation," Periwinkle says.

The chairs tilt forward then, and drop down into the darkness, accelerating toward the ground. Suddenly, we start to twist and turn as lights begin to stream in all directions, our screams filling the dark. The lights get brighter as we continue through the area before the chairs comes to a screeching halt, jolting us in our braces. As a pain wraps around my arms, I turn to Periwinkle to see a queasy look on his face.

It dissipates as he sits back into his chair. Bolts of light take shape into an arrow pointing upwards, before disappearing, and the words NEXT LEVEL appear in its place. Before I can lean forward, Periwinkle places his hand onto my brace. After applying some pressure, it tightens around me, restricting me as the chairs start to vibrate.

"Hang on!" Periwinkle yells.

The chair rocket upwards into the darkness and farther away from the glimmering words. Shortly after, the words fade into oblivion, forcing all my attention upwards into the direction of our movement. Suddenly, the darkness splits open, revealing a glimmering light, which gets brighter as we get closer. The chairs continue to speed upward, and I wrap my hands wrap tighter around the brace as my teeth clench. We then feel the speed slow down as it makes its way through the opening. Once we pass out of the darkness, the chairs stop roughly as the floor shuts. I blink, finding us once more on the outskirts of the three rings.

The first ring is to the left, where clowns remain sitting at their desks, writing around a single door. Next to it, a red circle surrounds an empty section of brain with lights moving all about. My legs are wobbly as Periwinkle and I gingerly unbuckle from the chairs and walk toward the third ring. After a couple of steps, he pauses, glitter raining down from above the opening.

"What is that?" I ask, watching the layers of sparkling specks wave downwards.

"The creation classroom," Periwinkle replies.

I wonder what might be inside the ring as I walk toward the opening. Before my eyes, the glitter stops in place, and ice begins to form. Before long, the ice creeps together, blocking the way.

"How am I supposed to get in?" I ask, making my way closer to the barrier. My hand brushes against the side of the ice, hoping for it to fall apart.

"You've got to have the drive, because if you don't, bad things will happen," Periwinkle replies, stepping up to the ice barrier next to me. Then, before my eyes, he steps through the solid mass and disappears into the area beyond the ice.

"Like what?" I ask, placing my hands up against the ice.

"You will get brain freeze," a voice replies from behind me. I glance back to see Periwinkle leaning on his bright staff. He twirls the staff about before pointing it off into the opposite direction. I turn to see an ice block with a brain hidden deep inside its core.

"What is that?" I ask, watching fog rise from the cube.

"Brain freeze is when you get a temporary loss of imagination due to cold temperatures," Periwinkle replies. We watch as the water puddles up underneath the brain when it suddenly melts. As the water puddles together, the brain remains floating for a moment, before it vanishes into the open space of the mind.

"I'm sure Guillermo doesn't like that," I say, turning my attention back to Periwinkle, only to find him on the other side of the once-frozen barrier. The pathway was clear, leaving not a drop of water in its wake, only the strange coloring of Periwinkle's outfit.

Periwinkle shakes his head before turning about and stepping deeper within the ring. I watch as he looks over his shoulder, smirking as he takes another step. Incredibly, he disappears and my jaw drops in surprise. 'I shouldn't be surprised by the crazy stuff going on in Guillermo's head,' I think to myself.

I then shrug, and step through the barrier after Periwinkle. Once beyond it, I look around for him, but there was no sign of him. I draw a deep breath down into my chest, allowing me to muster the confidence to take the next step. I close my eyes as I take another step, the bright lights fading into darkness. Before long, a tingling sensation covers my face, causing me to open my eyes. The sensation gives way to confusion as I find myself in unknown surroundings.

In front of me, sits a wooden square with a glob of saliva in the center, and a single metal bar hanging around the side. I lift my hands to wipe the last bits of blurriness from my eyes as I look at the room around me.

It is classroom, with desks all around a plain tile floor. The walls are an eggshell white and covered with giant dry-erase boards and an occasional learning poster. Then suddenly my eyes catch a glimpse of a giant figure in a suit and tie staring at me from across the room. His gray suit clashes horribly with his yellow tie, forcing me to turn my attention to his face and brown eyes. His expression, a mixture of sadness and pity, gives me relief as he makes his way back behind a shiny metal desk.

"Welcome to Creative 101," he says before sitting behind the desk.

As the creaking from his chair subsides, a projector screen drops down from the roof and rests over the board. Then a bright light shoots out from next to me, covering the screen with a giant square and the word *imagination.*

"Glad to see you made it," a voice whispers.

I turn my head to find Periwinkle, except this time it is a younger version of himself. Before I can answer him back, the teacher clears his throat and snaps his fingers with a thunderous bass. Our attention turns to him as the word *imagination* disappears and he stands up from his desk.

"With the beginning of every story, three questions must be answered," the teacher says, turning as the projector changes. The word *character* appears in a bold lettering. "First is a general thing that is a favorite for an individual, in this case Guillermo," the teacher continues.

"You mean like animals?" Periwinkle chimes, causing the teacher to turn back. Once more the word *character* fades from view, allowing the word *animal* to take over.

"Indeed Periwinkle, however, maybe someone who hasn't invaded my creation class a dozen times can answer," the teacher scorns, causing him to droop back into his desk. The teacher then shifts his gaze onto me as I struggle to digest the answer to his question. With little thought, I lift my arm into the air, causing the teacher to nod his head.

"How does a general thing allow you to create a story?" I ask, allowing my arm to drop back down to my desk.

The teacher rubs the sides of his face before turning around to see the word as it remains on the screen behind him. Suddenly, a light bulb appears above his head, shining brightly in the dimness of the classroom. "If a writer is passionate about something, such as animals, the story has a better chance of being completed."

Behind him, the word *animal* vanishes and a collage of animal images appears on the screen. Animals of all types and sizes make up a barrage of images, catching our attention. I then watch as the teacher examines the images before he lifts his finger and points toward a picture of a bear to the far left. The image starts to glow, swelling in size as the remaining pictures sink beneath it. I watch the as the other images disappear, leaving the single bear remaining on a black screen. It expands in size before shifting in direction, so it faces the classroom. Once in place, the image freezes as the teacher turns his attention back to Periwinkle and me. "Let us use this bear for example. Can you come up with a name?"

I turn to Periwinkle, but he appears to be asleep at his desk, forcing me to come up with something. My eyes shift to the image to stare face-to-face with the bear as it remains on the screen.

"Beary?" I whimper out.

The teacher lets out a tiny chuckle before covering his mouth to prevent any further sound. Next to me, Periwinkle lifts his head up from the desk with a grin from ear to ear. Struggling to contain his laughter, he moves his hand over to his other arm and then pinches himself, leaving a red mark along his white skin. The grin fades away just as a single tear rolls down his cheek.

"Okay, so we have established the main character to be Beary the bear," the teacher says, causing me to turn back to him. Behind him, a white shirt appears over his brown fur with the word Beary written on it. "Next thing we must answer is the location of the story."

"What do you mean?" I ask, keeping one eye on the bear behind the teacher in case something else changes with it.

"Like urban, rural, land, water, etc.," the teacher says as suddenly the black background begins to change to match the various landscapes available.

Once the final one flashes, the screen returns to black, leaving the lone bear image by itself. My eyes quickly shift to the teacher when he takes a couple steps back toward his desk. He then reaches behind as a metallic clang rings out, the sound of a drawer being pulled from its sleeve. After a moment of silence, another loud clang fills the room, and his hand reappears. Inside his hand, a small cardboard box sits atop his palm as he makes his way into the center of the classroom.

"Is that a box?" Periwinkle asks, causing the teacher to pause. He nods his head, kneeling and placing the box down upon the sturdy tile.

"Have you learned nothing from this class?" the teacher replies.

"Just don't think I have ever seen you use a box in your lessons," Periwinkle answers as we continue to watch the teacher place his hands along the lip of the box.

"Yes, well sometimes you think outside the box," the teacher says, opening the box. Before either of us can reply, the teacher steps back, allowing a darkness from inside to splatter across the walls.

My eyes spin around, looking for any sign of light, only able to make out the slight outline of Periwinkle. I then watch as the walls around me start to manifest buildings, extending through the roof. Between each one, alleyways creep around the corners along with food carts of various street foods. Before long, pedestrians appear along the fronts of the buildings and they begin to walk from the front of the room to the back. Underneath their feet, an asphalt street appears on the tiles. With the entire setting set, sunshine begins to beam down from out of the crevices in between the buildings.

"Is this the urban setting?" Periwinkle asks, causing me to look over at him.

Before anyone can answer, a horn blares, causing us to turn around. Suddenly my eyes widen as I see two bright lights fast approaching us. The vehicle gets within inches of us, and I shut my eyes, bracing for an impact that doesn't come.

"Woah, this is cool," a voice says, causing my eyes to reopen.

Before I can speak, another set of lights appear and charge toward me. The vehicle storms through us like a specter and heads for the other side of the wall. My eyes, struggling to take in the entire scene, blur slightly, which causes me to rub them. Once the blurriness clears, the sunlight fades and leaves moonlight reflecting on the windows of the skyscrapers.

The glistening specks of light on the buildings are hidden as a figure causes the illusion around us to tremble. Before him, a door opens, revealing the innards of a lobby from which he steps out of. Just as he steps into the light, the shadowy figure reveals himself to be the teacher. I then turn to Periwinkle who looks back at me with our eyes wide open. We look back to the teacher, who proceeds into the center of the street. Passing between the speeding cars, the teacher makes it safely before stopping on the trail of white lines.

"Now let's see if the grass is greener on the other side," the teacher says with bass in his voice.

As his voice echoes, the buildings crumble toward the ground and the cars shatter into the street. The tiny particles fade away, returning the room to a blanket of darkness. Through the silence, the sound of a bird chirping enters the room, causing us to look around in the darkness. We watch a strip of light appear in the molding of the walls, which grows larger with each passing moment. As more space reveals itself, my eyes catch sight of a blue sky with trees that reach high into the air. A large red building appears behind the green trees. A field of green as far as the eye can see stretches behind the red building, except for the patches of brush breaking up the monotony of grass. Beneath our feet, the grass extends, connecting all sides of the room.

"I get it now," Periwinkle says as the red building zooms into focus.

Pushing past the trees, our eyes start to take in the details of the building and the various colors that sit behind the bold red that caught our eyes. White lines guide every edge and corner, and specks of brown lay throughout from the wood peeking through the old paint. Suddenly, the red peels back, revealing a large white door with a split down the middle. It creaks open, allowing us to see the shadowy space behind it as it comes into the light. Once it reaches the end, various farm animals appear, running through the room and off toward the horizon of the image around us.

From out of the darkness, a rumble shakes the ground and a metallic vehicle roars. It explodes onto the scene, revealing a vibrant green tractor with its shiny wheels rumbling around the grass. Behind the wheel is a single man in blue overalls, with a cowboy hat carefully sitting on his head. His fresh face reflects the light from above, causing us to struggle to make out much more, until suddenly he places his foot down upon a pedal. The tractor takes off, sending soil high into the sky.

It nearly tumbles over before making its way toward a nearby hill near, which the animals had sped toward. Just before he can disappear out of sight, the man lifts his hat into the air and then accelerates, allowing the shining light to erase his visage.

A stream of smoke suddenly takes over the sky, causing us to follow it back. As we turn about, the smoke grows darker as we see embers erupt from the cracks inside the roof of the barn. From within the darkness inside, a red glow appears and smoke swirls from out the doorway.

"This isn't good," I say, watching as the red glow escalates into whipping flames.

They spread throughout the framework, peeling the red paint back and replacing it with peaks of fire. Ash falls from the heavens, covering the grass below, and a sudden darkness catches our attention. Shifting our stares, we watch as enormous clouds block out the sun, sending the entire area into a gray shade.

Fat raindrops start to come down in waves all around the field of grass. It falls upon the barn, causing a dance of fire and water to take place. The rain seeps within the openings of the building as the fire simmers down. The core of reddish-orange flames dissipates, overcome by the moisture. Once the final ember fades away, the remaining sounds of water falling causes peace to fill the field. After a couple moments, the rain weakens and the clouds above lighten and move out to the fields over the hill. The sun returns, revealing the worn-out exterior of the barn as water continues to slide off the tilting beams of wood.

After the sky fully clears, the rumbling sound returns, turning our attention back over to the hill in the distance. My eyes catch sight of a single speck, which grows larger with every passing second, until finally I can tell it is the tractor gathering speed toward us. Exhaust trails behind it as the tractor shreds through the fresh grass back to the barn. As he gets closer, the farmer slows down as he passes by me, allowing me to get a good look at him.

My eyes widen in disbelief when I recognize the driver to be none other than the teacher. He stops just shy of the barn's shadow and gets off the seat as the wheels come to a rest. As the smoke fades away, the teacher makes his way over to the barn and places his hand on the crispy wood. His lips shrivel when suddenly the barn implodes into the ground, sending a wave of dust into the air. Inch by inch, the sky darkens as the teacher turns his attention upward. Once the sun is out of view, he shifts his attention back in our direction.

The teacher allows the dust to settle before the scene goes dark. A light begins to beam downwards from the sky and onto the floor in front of us, revealing the tile floor underneath the façade of grass. The teacher steps forward then, in his suit and tie once more.

A New Scene

"What's next?" Periwinkle asks as I remain silent.

"Let me show you," the teacher says, twisting as he extends his hands into the surrounding darkness.

As we watch on, his hands return with a large metal object with a porcelain fixture attached to the side of it. With a nob on each side of a large faucet, the remainder of the sink-like object was a simple metal fixture. He turns back to us, struggling to hold it up.

"You're going to make the setting a kitchen sink?" Periwinkle asks.

The teacher lets out a smile when suddenly he lets go of it, causing the sink to fall to the ground. Before it can crash into the floor, the sink stops in mid-air, allowing a section of cabinetry to appear below it. As it molds around the sink, the teacher turns and watches. "You've seen everything else during my tenure in this classroom."

"It's definitely different," Periwinkle answers with a smirk.

The teacher nods as he shifts his attention back to the sink, lifting his hands over each of the nobs. He places them directly on top and wraps his fingers around the grooves making up their edges. He then twists both and the faucet starts to rumble and shake. It stops, causing the teacher to look all around the room. We do the same, seeing nothing but darkness around the faint outlines of the boards surrounding us. Then, before we can turn out heads, we watch as water rains down from the roof and begins to fill up the walls as if they are hollow. Swishing from side to side, the water rises upwards at a substantial rate.

Watching as it continues to rise, my eyes wander behind me to see the water crashing about in the wall. Curiously, I press my hand against the wall, watching the water continue to rise. I then watch as the water makes its way all the way to the molding at the edge of the roof. Once it was there, the water slides forward onto the roof, filling up the open space above us. Surrounding us, I look over at Periwinkle who keeps his eyes glued to the roof. "What is happening?"

"I think it's setting the scene," Periwinkle replies, cautiously keeping his eyes upon the swaying water above us.

I stare back at the water as it fills up the space above us. Once complete, the water becomes still as we look around the room.

"What is that?" Periwinkle asks as I look over at him, finding him pointing downward to the black floor.

Just as I look down, a sparkle of light appears from within the depths of darkness beneath us. It grows as it approaches the room. I then catch sight of a massive creature with a pair of large fins as it propels itself through the water. Its pale complexion contrasts with the blue surroundings, allowing us to see it in its entirety. However, before I can get a good look, the creature charges toward the floor and then explodes through it. It then swims through the open air, revealing itself to us. It was an average size whale with a charcoal black eye on both sides and a single horn upon its snout.

"If I remember correctly, this is called a narwhal," I reply as the whale slams into the roof and takes off through the water above us. We silently watch the whale disappear into the shadows of the water.

"Within different settings, various challenges must be overcome," a familiar voice says.

"Such as?" Periwinkle replies.

"For example, in an underwater scene, one must overcome the challenges of breathing and other explosive items such as mines," the teacher replies.

We watch as, from all around the room, black spheres appear with thorn-like appendages sticking out of them. From beneath each one, links of chains hang downward into the depths, along with green algae growing on the links. As we watch, the current shifts, sending one of the mines into another, which sends a loud clang echoing through the room.

As the mine bounces back, a small crack appears on the surface from the impact, which continues to expand. It spreads open and a small stream of bubbles seeps out into the open water. Then, suddenly, the mine explodes, sending a powerful shockwave into the surrounding waters. It spreads violently, ripping the other mines from their chains and sending them out to sea, leaving the chains to fall helplessly to the ground. The shockwave continues to push out in all directions, darkening the blue waters with chunks of metal from the mine.

We watch on as the water calms, allowing things to become motionless. I catch a glimpse of a ginormous shadow hiding beyond a thin layer of condensation. The blurry image contains several smaller shadows which hang down from it. "Can you see what that is?"

"I can't see anything behind that shield of moisture," Periwinkle replies, rising from his desk. He makes his way over to the wall where we saw the shadows and reaches his hand out toward the wall. Carefully, Periwinkle places it onto the wall and tries to wipe away the moisture. After leaving a trail of clear area in his wake, he then leans into the wall to get a better look.

"Can you see anything?" I ask him, attempting to get my own line of sight.

"Not a thing," Periwinkle replies, moving back from the wall.

After he takes a couple of steps back, a giant shadow swims in from the depths of the floor and drags its way up the wall. Proceeding upwards, large tentacles slide up against the surface, revealing large suction cups that sit within the membranes of the creature. They leave a residue on the wall. We follow the shadows upward, seeing it sway up and above the roof. Suddenly a beak appears from the base of the shadow and a set of giant eyes glitter in the darkness.

"I would suggest you return to your seat," the teacher cautions.

Periwinkle nods, running back to his seat as the monstrous eyes follow him. Safely back behind his desk, Periwinkle releases a deep breath. After a moment, Periwinkle looks up, causing me to do the same. Just in time, we watch as the creature releases its hold and launches upwards into the sea. Beneath it, a plume of black ink shoots out, encasing us in a sticky darkness. Unable to see, we strain to hear the swooshing waves as they make their way from one side to the other. Before long, the sound of waves fades away and the sound of a sea breeze takes over. Above us, a large circular object appears, along with tiny specks of light all around the roof. Peace and tranquility fill us as we watch the ground shift into rolling waves. From left to right, the waves' constant movement hypnotizes us and a massive shadow appears.

A large tail erupts from the surface and stands up into the open air. It then slams down, sending a misty eruption high into the air. As the drops fall, the tail sinks out of view, returning to the depths from which it came.

"With the idea of the sea, comes the dilemma of limitations," the teacher calls.

"Such as?" I ask, looking around at the growing waves in the distance.

"Every land has its pros and cons, with the sea being lack of air to breathe," the teacher says.

"What are the pros here?" I ask, watching as the growing waves crash together.

"Beauty, nature, and an unpredictable predictability," Periwinkle adds, causing me to look over at him.

"Can't you get that with land environments?" I ask, watching as the scenery starts to zip closer to the edge of the land.

"Yes, however, you can mold the sand into something greater," the teacher says.

"Like what?" I ask, continuing to watch braids of seaweeds crash into the space between the land and sea.

"A Castle," the teacher replies as suddenly the sand starts to quake.

The sand molds and erupts upwards, taking shape. Once it nearly touches the stars, the sand freezes still. It was a full-sized castle with doors and windows, with different shells making up the frame of the building. Then, from out of the main door, a figure steps out, the object in its hand shining in the light.

Looking closer, I can see a conch shell within his palm, but his body remains mysterious. After it takes a couple more steps from out of the shadows of the castle, we finally see that it's the teacher, holding a pristine orange and white conch shell within his grasp. Before we can open our mouths, the castle begins to break apart and sand rains down onto the crashing waves. Section by section, the castle crumbles away until finally there is nothing left. Once the sand settles, our eyes catch sight of the teacher.

"This is one of the issues with the fragileness of the sand," the teacher says, stepping out of the way to reveal the land behind him. The sand was undamaged and normal as the waves crash on the edge of the land.

"That giant castles can fall to the ground?" Periwinkle asks.

The teacher turns his head back before looking back down at the conch shell. He then lobs the shell in our direction. It flies through the wall, bouncing into the room and skittering across the ground in front of our desks.

We watch as the conch sparkles in the moonlight, the drops of saltwater evaporating off the shell. Before either of us can react, it starts to crumble and dissolve into the ground. Once the final speck falls away, we turn our attention back to the teacher.

To our surprise, we find nothing, just the sandy beach scene along with a single palm tree off on the horizon. Then, before our eyes, the moon overhead quickly slinks down toward the edge of the water. On the edge of the crashing waves, it drops away from our sight and the sky lights with an orange and red glow. Twisting around the small clouds, the colors light up the sky as rays of light appear. The sun begins to appear on the horizon, lighting up the once dark school with its warmth. With each passing second, the sky turns to blue as the sun climbs higher.

After a couple of moments, the sun pauses in the sky, allowing us to get a different look at a scene which was once set in the darkness of night. The once dreary atmosphere is now a beautiful setting for romance and positive vibes. The crashing waves are now relaxing as a section of foam extends outwards.

"Everything has more than one side," the teacher says between waves.

Our eyes shift to one of the side walls, revealing the teacher standing with his face facing the vast blue sky.

"You mean like a story?" I ask, causing the teacher to turn his head.

"Indeed," the teacher replies simply before looking back to the churning ocean.

Above our heads, the sparse clouds grow in number, hiding the blue sky. The change causes the teacher to look upwards as suddenly the world around us drops out of sight. It allows the sky to drop down to our level, causing the clouds to take over the floor. Above us, the sky the edge of the atmosphere keeps us separate from an expanse of stars. Between the clouds and space, the clouds suffocate the fleeting sunlight as the teacher turns around.

"What is this setting?" Periwinkle asks.

"This is the open sky where things with wings roam," the teacher replies, beginning to make his way toward the center of the room.

We watch as he kneels, causing a wispy cloud to rise higher into the space. He then extends his hands downward into the cloud's surface, splitting the cloud in half. On the other side of the cloud, he reveals a faint land of green with a mixture of browns along with a rainbow of other colors. After a moment, he moves his hands, allowing the cloud to re-solidify. He then looks over at us as I watch the clouds lift up over my ankles.

"What kinds of thing thrive in a setting like this?" I ask, looking at the teacher.

"Animals, machines, and angelic humans," the teacher replies, lifting his arms to the sky.

"How about pigs?" Periwinkle chimes in, causing the teacher to shift his attention.

"Depends how much ham they are carrying," the teacher replies with a grin.

Suddenly, the cloud beneath us gives way and the sight shifts once more. As we fall toward the ground, the details of the land start to grow as the space above gets farther away. Getting closer, the familiar coastline becomes clearer and the palm fronds merge into a blur. As we start to slow down, the sounds of the waves come over us, along with the sound of seagulls and peaceful nature. As we land with a crash, a wave of sand erupts and fans out around part of the room. I wipe my eyes before looking at the teacher standing behind the falling grains. However, before I can speak, everything around the room freezes and fades to black. I look over at Periwinkle, who looks surprised.

"What just happened?" I ask.

The teacher turns around silently and makes his way into the center of the room. As he does so, the room lights up once more, revealing the original setting of the classroom around us. Beneath me, the bland tiles return and take away any trace of the sceneries that have come and gone.

"We just had a power surge," the teacher replies.

"In the brain?" I ask, confused.

"I mean, we do run on brainpower," the teacher replies, watching as the lights above flicker before stabilizing.

"So wait, what is the third question that one must answer before writing a good story?" Periwinkle asks suddenly.

"That's right we haven't answered that yet," the teacher replies, placing his hand upon the patchy facial hair on his chin.

"So what is it?" I ask, watching him lower his hand back down to his side.

"The third question every writer needs to answer is what emotion are they looking to focus on," the teacher says.

I frown. *I mean, really? Emotions?* I thought to myself, *those just seem like things that can get in the way of a good story.* My attention shifts to the teacher and then to Periwinkle, both of whom staring in my direction. "Whats wrong?"

"You were misfiring," Perwinkle answers, looking over at the teacher.

"Yeah, sorry, I guess the whole emotions being important seemed a bit off," I reply as I look between them.

"Its true. But, think about everything you enjoy," the teacher says, making his way back over to his desk. I watch as he sits down, placing his hands on top.

"You mean like movies?" I reply, trying to think of some example of movies that I had seen from behind Guillermo's eyes. I had always thought of the amazing action scenes or the comedic wit of the actors and actresses. Never about the storyline or the emotion behind them.

"Especially movies where the main character must overcome odds in order to accomplish the final goal," the teacher replies. He tilts his head over to the side as he reaches down for a drawer. Pulling it out, he reaches in, pulling a variety of objects out to stack them on the desktop. He then fans them out before separating them by size. "Every genre, from romance to comedy, carries with it a certain set of emotions that they hope to bring out of the viewer," he continues.

"Like how, in particuliar?" I reply, sitting back in my desk as the teacher does the same in his chair.

The teacher looks over at the different cases before he picks up one from the middle of the row. He grabs it with his other hand and opens it up to reveal a shiny disc hiding inside. I watch him pop it free before spinning it around his finger. "The greatest movies establish a chain of emotions that can integrate other emotions along the way, as side stories come into view."

"So basically, you can write a love story and still have it carry with it a grain of fear and excitement," Periwinkle chimes in, causing me to shift my attention.

"In simple terms, yes," the teacher says. Before any of us can speak, the lights flicker once more, causing the teacher to throw down the disc in frustration.

"What's the matter?" I ask, listening to the teacher take a deep breath.

"Those surges mean that Guillermo is struggling to maintain his focus on a single idea," the teacher replies.

Suddenly, the lights go dim and flicker out. I turn to Periwinkle, who looks over at me in confusion, before we both look to the teacher as he stands from his chair.

"Well, brain power or not, emotions are the final major component to any successful story, along with character buildup and setting," the teacher continues.

As the final word leaves his lips, the door to the classroom explodes inwards, causing us to jump from our chairs. I struggle to understand what's happening as I look for the teacher. However, to my surprise, the teacher is gone, the pile of cases lying on the floor. Before I can move, a shadow appears, leading my eyes to a man surrounded by an orange glow from a lit torch. Despite the light, his face is hidden beneath a hooded cloak.

"Who are you?" Periwinkle asks, causing me to turn to look at him.

"My name is Omrel and I am a member of the Brainiacs," he bellows out from the shadows.

Omrel then turns around, lifting the torch into the air, allowing it to cast its light down the hall. With each step forward, more of the hall is revealed as the paint is stripped away, leaving bare stones in its wake. Torches light up along the walls, allowing the darkness to recede.

Periwinkle and I cautiously take a few steps toward the doorway in Omrel's shadow before I pause to look back into the classroom.

"Wonder where he went," I whisper, turning back to Periwinkle who shrugs before looking over at Omrel as he comes to a stop.

"Follow me to the next chamber," Omrel says in a bellowing voice.

With a gulp, we make our way to the doorway. Omrel is an imposing figure as he waits for us, his torch illuminating the bare stones. Periwinkle is first through the door, and he looks at me, the torchlight reflecting in his eyes as a smirk grows on his face.

"What is it?" I ask, gripping the side of the frame and peeking inside.

"You are afraid of what is coming next in your storyline," Periwinkle replies with a chuckle.

My face reddens and I angrily step through the door, a cold chill pushing through my shoe. I continue forward as Periwinkle watches me in amusement. All the while, my eyes remain on Omrel as he glances over his shoulder before looking back down the dark hall.

"So, what exactly are the Brainiacs?" I ask.

Omrel pauses, looking annoyed. "We are a who, not a what."

I watch as Periwinkle stops in his tracks as I step up next to him. Together, we watch as Omrel continues forward down the pathway, spreading the light to the very end, where a singular door stands tall against the cold walls. Omrel makes his way to the door before he stops in front of an oddly miscolored section. He turns and tilts the torch over to the wall, causing it to peel back into itself. As the rumbling of the shifting walls stops, Periwinkle and I take a few brisk steps before stopping near Omrel.

"Don't get too close to the Brain Drain," Omrel says, returning the torch back to his side.

I wonder about what is beyond this opening and what this Brain Drain truly is. I glance at Periwinkle, who is watching me carefully, before stepping up to the door. In front of me is a circular room with walls higher than any I'd ever seen from Guillermo's eyes. I shift my gaze toward the ground, finding a monstrous human-like creature sitting at the rim of what appears to be a swirling funnel. It doesn't acknowledge us; instead it keeps its focus upon a book in its hand.

The book seems to barely be held together by the spine as the pages line up between the front and back covers. I watch as the creature shifts its blue eyes down to the drain, which starts to unleash a vaccumn-like suction throughout the funnel. A plotting look appears on the creature's face as its eyes turn back to us. It then reaches one of its grotesque hands over to the front cover and turns it over, revealing the wording upon it.

"BloodMinazue," I say softly, watching as the creature looks down with a gleam in its eyes.

It then reaches down and pulls up a single empty page and sends it fluttering into the suction and down the funnel. Out of view, the grin turns to a smile as he rips another page from the bindings. After a swift tear, he then throws the next page into the opening.

"What is it?" a voice asks over my shoulder.

I look back to see Periwinkle staring heavily at the creature even as it continues to rip pages from the book.

"This is the original story that Guillermo wrote," Omrel replies as we look back just in time to see his head lower.

"Why is that creature ripping it apart?" Periwinkle asks as I turn back to the creature as it admires the disappearence of another page.

"This creature has a name," another voice blurts out. Our eyes shift around to the being to see it staring back at us. Both eyes, one blue and one brown, stare at us as it places the remnants of the book onto the floor.

"Okay, so what is it?" I ask, causing the creature to shift its eyes to me.

"Mozen, and I'm not destroying this book," replies the creature, wiping the tangles of curly hair away from its face.

"So what are you doing then?" Periwinkle asks.

"I am merely storing the characters in this story for future uses," Mozen replies as the book shreds into thin air.

"I'm sorry, you are doing what?" I ask, watching Mozen stand up on top of stringy legs above his massive feet.

"See, when stories fail or have a hinderance, it is best to take the important aspects of it and store them for future endeavors," Mozen replies, following the shreds of the book as they swirl through the air.

Our eyes watch as his head sways with every twist and turn of the pages until finally they evaporate from sight. Mozen turns to us as we remain silent in the doorway before he shifts his attention over our shoulders.

"Come you two, we must remain on the storyline," Omrel says, breaking our attention as we turn around to him. We watch as he aims the torch downward to the stone ground, revealing the word *storyline* along the ground. I look on, the word repeating itself both in front of us and behind us. Omrel pulls back the torch, causing the words to vanish.

Before we can speak a word, a rumbling shudders underneath our feet before fading away as things return to normal. I look to see Omrel staring behind us, causing us to turn back to find that the opening where Mozen stood is no longer there. No trace of the door remains, just a single flowing wall as the stones mesh together. I then turn back around to find Omrel beginning to take another step down the hall.

"What happened to him?" Periwinkle asks before I can.

I watch as Omrel pauses, turning his attention to Periwinkle as he stands next to me.

"Mozen has joined the others in storage," Omrel replies as Periwinkle and I exchange a look.

"How is that?" I ask.

"Mozen was indeed a version of a character within the very story he was tearing apart," Omrel says before turning his attention back down the hallway.

The Brainiacs

We watch Omrel continue down the hall as the very end begins to light up. As the light touches the corners of the hall, a wooden door appears in the center of the wall. On both sides, a golden disc sits just beyond the edge of the framework, with a darker than usual shadow above it. As we come closer, I can see tinier rose-colored gems lining along the rim of the discs as the light breaks the darkness. A dark wooden branch sits inside them, casting a reflection onto the wall behind it.

Meanwhile, the door starts to gain detail, from the grains of wood to the faint number three laying on top of its surface. The handle to the left contains a fake handprint, engraved along the knob. Omrel breaks my gaze by reaching for the brass handle as it stiffens beneath his grasp.

"Now that you have heard the three mandatory questions for any story, we approach the conclusion," Omrel says, turning his attention to us.

As we remain frozen feet away, I watch as Omrel's fingers tighten and a jolt shakes the door loose from its hinges. A stream of smoke escapes from the door, getting larger as the door opens. Once it was wide open, the smoke lessens as it leaves a familiar dark space with lights shooting from one side to another. Struggling to comprehend what we are seeing, we watch as Omrel removes his hand and makes his way into the darkness.

After watching him disappear, I look to Periwinkle, who shrugs before taking his first step toward the open doorway. As I continue to watch, Periwinkle walks through into the darkness and disappears from sight.

"I guess I am next," I whisper out loud.

However, just as I begin to take my first step toward the doorway, a circle of light appears from its depths. Flickering and growing, the light gets larger as it approaches the edge of the darkness. Breaking free, a torch floats from out of the darkness and makes its way to the golden disc on the left side. It tilts forward and sends the wooden stick into flames before heading to the other side. Once there, it does the same to the other, causing it to burst into flames.

As both wooden sticks smolder upwards, the original torch cools and goes out as it crashes to a smoking heap on the ground. Stepping around the dead torch, I look back to the glittery darkness inside the doorframe. Taking in a single deep breath, my feet lift one by one closing the distance between the doorway and myself. Just as I step inside, I pause, placing my hand around the wooden side of the frame.

I watch the darkness as it waves around the opening, the prismatic lights bouncing back and forth. I then brace my hand before using it to propel myself forward, out of the light of the torches. The darkness overtakes me with no resistance, and my eyes struggle to keep sight of the pathway in order to keep track of Periwinkle and Omrel. After a moment, the darkness lessens, allowing me to see two shadows standing just beyond my reach. Taking a couple more steps, I begin to see them as they turn their attention toward me. "Thank you for waiting for me."

"No problem, the Spaces of No Ideas can be overwhelming," Omrel replies, his eyes glittering with the surrounding twinkles of light.

"Is there anyway to light up the space like the dark hallway?" I ask.

"A bright idea," Omrel replies. As his words resonate outward, the darkness starts to weaken and chunks of the area become illuminated. Suddenly, an enormous source of energy appears overhead, destroying the remnants of the darkness and allowing us to see clearly.

I find myself back inside the room where I had met Periwinkle, along with the Three Rings of Thought. Even though the entire room is empty, they still remain in front of us as if we had been here all along. "How did you get rid of the darkness?"

"I did nothing, it was all him," Omrel replies as he points over to the corner of the room.

Our eyes shift to find a skinny figure with a pair of brown eyes beneath a mop of blonde hair. A loose, blue button-down shirt matches his khaki shorts. He remains still against the wall of the room.

"Who is that?" I ask, watching as the figure turns about and disappears into the hall outside of our sight.

"His name is Will, and with his power you can create anything when you have the drive," Omrel replies.

"So where is he going?" Periwinkle asks.

Before I can turn, the lights surrounding us shut off, causing a deathly darkness to move in. "What is going on?"

No one speaks, leaving the darkness to absorb our prescence, when suddenly a maniacal laugh echoes through the room, causing me to look all around. Before long, the laugh fades and a scream rings out from the room as the lights return and I realize Periwinkle is missing.

"Where did he go?" Omrel asks.

"See, one thing that your ringmaster friend forgot to menton is that every storyline needs an antagonist," a voice bellows into the room.

"Is that where you come in?" I ask, continuing to look for any sign of my lost companion. Without a reply, another round of manical laughter sounds just as Omrel approaches from behind.

"I was afraid of this," Omrel whispers.

"What is it?" I reply.

"Its more like a whom," Omrel replies.

"What he means to say is that my name is Manuel, and I'm the anti-hero aspect of your storyline!" Manuel yells.

"Okay, so where have you taken Periwinkle?" I ask, continuing my search for any trace of either Periwinkle or this Manuel. Hearing nothing, Omrel and I continue to look all about when a scream rings out from the silence.

"Periwinkle is fine, just overly dramatic," Manuel's voice rings out.

"My legs," a voice similar to Periwinkle's cries out.

"Give him back!" I yell.

"I will, once you find me on the train of thought," Manuel replies when suddenly a door mysteriously appears next to us along the wall.

Before either of us can reach for the handle, the door swings open as the wall expands in all directions. Suddenly, the silence and bland lighting of the room gives way to a metallic sensation, along with the chugging of mechanical vehicles coming and going. The trains park at the stations as tiny figures wait for them on a wooden platform.

I continue to stare as the doors, which are open wide to allow the figures inside, but a loud creaking sound slams the doors closed. Bright lights shine from out of the rear, allowing the train to charge forwards down glowing tracks. Following it off into the periphery, my eyes look over at Omrel who follows my gaze.

"Welcome to the Brain Station," Omrel replies, lifting his hand upwards to reveal a glowing pathway between us and the platform.

"What is this place?" I ask, watching as Omrel starts to walk between the lines of glowing lights.

"This is where thoughts go to be placed in the different sectors of the brain," Omrel replies, looking back as he continues on the glittery pathway. Taking a step onto the wooden platform, his foot leaves a shining footprint, which fades into thin air after a moment. Once on the platform, he looks back to me as I turn my attention to the pathway that now separates us.

I lift up my left foot and place it down onto the speckling ground, and then my right, discovering it to be as safe as my current location. With some hesitation, I walk over quickly, watching Omrel take a step forward. As I get to the end, I watch as Omrel continues onto the empty platform as a beaming light appears down the tracks. Stepping off, I turn back to watch the pathway dissolve, piece by piece, until it unblocks the way. Turning back, Omrel stands behind a yellow line drawn on the platform when he looks over at me.

"The train is here," Omrel says, turning his attention toward the oncoming light. It grows larger as it approaches and the horn signals its arrival. As its brakes tighten, a stream of smoke ruptures from each side, twisting around the beam of light pluming from the chimney.

Watching on, I unknowningly make my way towards him as the door slides out from its locked position. Breaking the lines along the side of the frame, the door reveals a pathway that splits into two directions inside the cabin.

"Come aboard," Manuel's voice sounds out before clicking off the intercom.

"Guess we should," Omrel whispers, taking his first step toward the metal lip of the cabin. Once inside, he glances back at me and beckons me to follow.

I take a deep breath and make my way forward as I watch Omrel step out of the way to allow me some room at the entrance. Once inside, the door shuts swiftly, nearly clipping the back of my pants as they lock automatically. As the mechanism clicks into place, the intercom clicks on, a field of static fading into silence.

"Welcome aboard the Supporting Details Express," Manuel says, just before the intercom clicks out once again. The train jumps forward as the brakes release, causing us to brace ourselves upon the bar going from side to side.

Turning our attention to the two pathways, I look to Omrel as he seems to ponder between the two. "I'm going to the left."

"Why that way?" Omrel asks, watching as I make my way toward the left pathway.

"Because Guillermo is left handed!" I reply back with a smirk, continuing to make my way down the slim hallway.

Passing by the first open doorway, sounds ring out in repetition, causing me to peek from around the frame. Inside, the floor gives way to a sandy bottom up to the window. On one side is a muscular man with a massive frame, wearing ripped pants and a chestplate with a matching helmet covering his head and neck. The metallic armor outmatches the fighter on the other side. The man, scrawny and weak, struggles to keep his attention on the brute in front of him as his eyes keep getting sidetracked to the cheering crowd all around them. I watch as, with one vicious swipe of an iron sword, the shaking mace is knocked from his hands. The large man kicks out the flimsy legs of the scrawny man, causing him to drop to his knees in the sand.

He grins, revealing his yellow teeth as he aims his heavy sword at the other man's face. Before anything more can happen, the door slides shut, snuffing out all of the sound from the other side. That is when my eyes catch sight of the door and the wording in the center of it.

"Villian takes round 1," Omrel says, scaring me and causing me to jump toward the door.

Once my heart beat returns to normal, I turn back with my hand onto my chest, seeing Omrel standing with his head turned to the side. Before I can say anything, the sound of the intercom clicking on causes us to pause.

"Now that the villian has taken round 1, the next door hangs on the hero's perserverance," Manuel says, clicking out shortly after his last word. The crowd's cheering suddenly returns, except this time it is farther away.

I turn toward the doorway just feet away, listening to the crowd cheering as it starts to get louder as I step closer. The chanting blurs into nonsense as I arrive to the opening to see the scene where the other left off. The two fighters remain in their positions, when suddenly the attacker lifts his sword high up into the air.

As his muscles flex, the sword waves in the air and the other fighter looks on with his hands against the sandy surface. Then, just as the sword slinks backward, the man's hands squeeze against the ground and swing upwards, sending a spray of sand into the attacker's face. The sword slumps downward as the attacker struggles to regain his sight while the other rolls to safety. With his opponent blinded temporarily, I watch as he reaches out for the mace before wrapping his hand around its wooden grip. He turns back just in time to watch the attacker wipe the last grains from out of his eyes.

In utter rage, the attacker's face reddens and he regrips his sword and places it out in front of him. Meanwhile, the other man swiftly takes a couple steps in front of me to where I can only see his back. The attacker then angrily unleashes a strike, but the man dodges out of the way. I then watch as the attacker shifts his attention back to the man as he now stands on the far side of the cabin. Letting out a grunt just underneath the roar of the crowd, the attacker steps forward, kicking up sand with each lift of his foot.

The two men continue to step sideways, waiting for the other to make the first move, when suddenly both stop in their tracks as their feet sink just below the top level of sand. Suddenly, the attacker jumps toward the man with his sword raised high, attempting to deliver a strike, when it is met by the thick body of the metallic mace. As the clang rings out over the roaring crowd, the attacker backs off as the other attempts to shake the feeling back into his fingers.

Seeing an opportunity, the attacker this time charges forward and unleashes a barrage of blows in all directions, causing the man to try to defend each one. With each collision, the man's feet stumble back a half step as the other attempts to gain the advantage. Just before another strike can land, the man twists out of the way and watches as the attacker angrily kicks sand high into the air. As the vein in his neck begins to show, he turns around to see the man lifting the mace in defense once more. I watch as the attacker lifts up his blade toward his face as his eyes shift. Assuming his gaze is taking in the impact marks, I watch the attacker stare back at the man. Beads of sweat slide down their figures, the two men's breathing slowing as I watch on.

Suddenly, the attacker storms forward, swinging the sword dramatically around as he roars. Just before he can unleash a strike, the man throws the mace high into the air as he rolls underneath. Struggling to maintain his balance, the attacker wobbles about as we watch the man grasp his mace just before it can land in the sand. Then, within a blink of an eye, the man spins about and slams the blunt end into the attackers back.

The attacker flies forward, crashing into the sand, sending up a wave of dust around him. Our eyes shift to the man as he exhales, watching as the attacker remains motionless on the ground. However, after a moment, the attacker rises back to his feet just as the man lowers his mace to his side. The attacker's face is coated with sand as he looks around until he locates his sword's hilt poking out of the ground. He then grabs it as his other hand lays palm down upon the clumping sand. Then, using the sand as leverage, the attacker lifts himself up with a stumble as the man watches. Barely able to maintain his stance, the attacker aims his sword at the man as the sand continues to fall from his face.

Then in a surprise move, the attacker unclips his chestplate and lets it fall onto the ground, revealing his muscular body. The crowd roars in applause as a large bruise upon his back appears. Then the crowd goes silent as the attacker's blade drifts upward, and the man's eyes follow it to the blue sky. The man grips tightly his mace with his other hand as the attacker lets out a primitive howl. Then, just as both men sink their feet into the ground, the scene falls silent. Not a whisper or a random clap, just silence, which gives way to a familiar mechanical screech.

I turn back toward the door as it slides shut and once more locks in the place. Stepping back, the door seals around the frame and I turn back to Omrel. Unable to speak, another loud click rings, sending our eyes upwards.

"Edge for round two goes to the defender," Manuel's voice rings out.

"What's next?" I yell, hands waving in the air.

My eyes search around for the next source, only to find the sealed two doorways that gave me the first two rounds. I look to Omrel when suddenly a loud screech reveals an open doorway just to our left. From out of the faint darkness, a sparkling light shines into the hallway. Ready for round three, both of us cautiously make our way towards it. We look inside the room where, to our surprise, we find a normal cabin. Nothing out of the ordinary, from the bland walls to the plain seats on both sides. The material of each chair contains a single rose embossed into the middle of the fabric.

"Are you ready for the finale?" Manuel's voice sounds, revealing his true figure from out of the shadows.

The man, tanned from head to toe, is wearing clothes similar to Periwinkle's, but his white suit is wrinkle-free and blends perfectly into the plain scene all about. In his left hand he holds the brim of a top hat.

Before I can say a word, Manuel sits down on one of the seats on the left side and turns his attention to me. With my hand gently up against the metallic frame, I make my way inside, trying not to stare at him. I turn my attention to the chairs on the other side before taking a seat on one of them. As I get comfortable, I look to Omrel, who stays between the two sides of the doorway. "Come inside and take a seat."

"That's okay, I'm going to find the dining car and hope they have pizza," Omrel replies, smirking as he takes a step back into the dim hallway.

I watch as he turns left and walks off into the darkness, leaving Manuel and me alone inside the cabin. As I continue to take in my surroundings, my eyes shift around the room and I catch a glimpse of the window. Outside the glass plate are sparkling lights and twisting darkness which stretches from one end to the other.

"Enjoying the depths of Deep Thought?" Manuel asks, causing me to break my stare and turn my attention back to him.

"Deep Thought?" I ask, watching as Manuel shifts to the seat closer to the window as he peaks out of it.

"An area of Guillermo's mind that he goes to when he isn't daydreaming," Manuel replies, smirking as he turns to me.

"So what is the finale?" I ask, shifting in my chair as Manuel does the same.

"It's the conclusion to the very final action of the story," Manuel replies.

"What is the conclusion?" I ask.

"The eventual return of Periwinkle," Manuel replies, pointing a finger out the window.

As my attention shifts toward it, the darkness suffocates out the last bits of light as we continue to move faster along the tracks. As I stare into the darkness, a multi-colored glow comes into the depths, causing me to stare at the fluctuating colors. The lights grow brighter until suddenly a flat shadow appears along the ground. Before long, two words surrounded by lightbulbs of various colors appear.

"Secondary Traits," I say aloud, turning my attention momentarily to Manuel, who continues to stare heavily into the world beyond.

"This is the part of the journey that is used to help Guillermo decide the narration aspects of his storyline," Manuel replies.

I watch as the light from the sign passes faintly into the shadows and the darkness starts to peel back from a far greater light source. As the ring of light approaches, the colors of the train are revealed, a rainbow of red shades between streaking blues along the edges.

Coming closer, the light passes over us and reveals a man along with four makeshift walls. Each one is labeled with a number as he stands confident to the side with a plain brown book in his hands. His clothing, a baby blue robe, hangs just over his gray sandals, which match the gray undershirt peaking out under his top layer. His black hair is combed over to the side, allowing his youthful face to be revealed. Finally, the train drops to a snail's pace and I watch the man turn his attention toward us. His face is stoic and cold as he shifts toward the structures and the light above shifts along with him.

Keeping his eyes on the walls, I watch as the man takes a couple of steps away before turning back around. He lifts the book in his hands and extends his arm behind him. Once his arm is fully extended, the man swings his arm forward sending the book spinning in the direction of the structures. The book spirals toward a wall as we watch in anticipation. With a thunderous impact, the book erupts through the back of it as it continues to churn its way toward the second. With little resistance, the book saws its way through, sending chunks of rock crashing to the floor. As the two tumble to the ground, the third also proves no match as the book starts to tilt uncontrollably.

"Will it break the fourth wall?" Manuel asks, causing me to look over before returning to watch the spiraling book make its approach.

Its spinning slows slightly as the space between it and the wall shrinks. Finally the book strikes the wall, slamming to a stop before falling to the ground. The book suddenly returns to the man's possesion as all of our eyes return to the final wall, which trembles slightly as a couple of pebbles fly out of the back.

"Guess not," I reply, looking over at Manuel who frowns at the sight of the still-standing wall.

"Darn, and I was really hoping for a fourth wall break," Manuel replies.

Before I can reply, the wall starts to rumble and large crevices appear along the face, to our surprise. Manuel's frown lifts to a smile as larger chunks peel off and smash into bits around the base. Suddenly, a gaping hole appears in the center, sending a crack upwards as the base becomes unstable. It tumbles to the ground, causing the man to open the book in his hands. He then pulls out a writing instrument and turns to one of the page inside. After scribbling about, he pulls it back and looks back at us as the train speeds up.

"Fourth wall break!"the man yells before disappearing into the thickening glow of the light above. As his voice fades away, the train continues forward, leaving the bright lights behind.

I then turn to Manuel to find him already sitting up straight along the wall of the cabin. "What is so important about the fourth wall?"

Manuel looks over and rubs his chin as he stares above my head. "It's rare for a storyline to break into the fourth wall."

"Why is that?" I ask.

"It involves getting the audience, or in this case readers, a deeper connection," Manuel replies, turning toward the other half of the cabin.

My eyes follow suit, seeing nothing out of the ordinary. I turn back to watch Manuel continue to stare. "What are you doing?"

"Nothing," Manuel replies, winking before he shifts back into a forward position in the chair.

Thinking nothing of it, and feeling a jolt of speed, my eyes make their way toward the window and the encompassing darkness.

"Are you ready for the next lesson?" Manuel asks.

Keeping my body leaning toward the window, I peek around to see him staring a hole into the window. "I'm guessing I have no choice."

Manuel nods as he points toward the window, causing my attention to shift to the darkness as the train once again comes to a still.

The Next Lesson

My eyes are met with three shadows flashing across the grounds as they enter the rim of light. As the train continues, I try to get to get a closer look at the sources. However, darkness is as far as the eye can see except for a sprinkle of glitter coming out of its depths. The closer we got, the less positive I am over the idea of what is to come, when suddenly three beams of light shoot down from above. Each one lights up a section of space, revealing a single being within its glorious aura. The one closest, a mere few feet away, watches with his brown eyes as the train comes closer. Then with a lift of his hand, I feel the train slow as our cabin creeps towards him. I watch as the figure lowers his hand just as our cabin stops in front of him, revealing him to be someone quite familiar.

Before my eyes, Omrel appears in his attire, carrying a crimson red plate with an enormous slice of pizza drooping over the edge. Its cheese barely holds on as Omrel stares, a drop of tomato sauce slipping to the ground. Something is different about his robe as I spot a glittering number one across the fabric on his chest. His eyes shift back onto the cabin, widening when he spots me looking back at him. Then, just as he starts to open his mouth, the two beams behind him make their way forward, revealing two other figures whom I had never seen before. They both stand on either side of Omrel, revealing numbers of their own, a two and three respectively.

The number two is carried by a thin, yet average, man whose skin darkens from the light above. His face is masked by his stringy red curls, and his blue shirt is wrinkled all the way to the sleeves. His face appears innocent and wrinkle-free, and he attempts to brush his bangs away from his pale blue eyes. The top of his head barely reaches Omrel's broad shoulders. He turns his head to Omrel as his lanky arms droop downward to his sides, hands tucked into the pockets of camo shorts.

On the other side, number three appears to be a much taller man with an average build wearing a short-sleeved green shirt. It matches the forests that I had once seen beyond Guillermo's eyes. The man jokingly places his arm upon Omrel's shoulder as Omrel looks back, chomping on his first bite of pizza. He then turns back to the cabin, revealing black eyes.

"I don't think you should be showing off to tourists," Number Two speaks out in a bellowing voice. Number Three drops his arms, his face falling in disappointment.

"Who are those three?" I ask, turning to Manuel.

"This is your next lesson," Manual replies, keeping his eyes on the three figures outside our window.

"What is it?" I ask, causing Manuel to tilt his head back before looking at me.

"Deciding between which perspective you want to write from," Manuel replies.

My sight shifts from him to the three outside as they continue to stare at us.

"What's wrong?" I ask, watching as the three begin to shift their glances amongst themselves.

"Number Three thinks that the audience needs to be quiet so the three perspectives can figure out which is best," a deep voice speaks out. I then watch as Number Three lifts up his arm with a finger pointing up to the ceiling.

"My apologies," I reply, watching as Number Three looks upward.

"Number Three accepts the apology of the odd gentleman peering from the train cabin," the voice shouts out once again.

I sit back as suddenly a rumbling starts to overcome the silence in the room. Our eyes shoot upwards as a whistling sound rings through our ears as the rumbling fades away. Then, abruptly, a massive object crashes down into the darkness behind them, causing the three figures to look back. As they stare into the darkness, the three lights shift off the figures and aim onto the object, revealing it to everyone. Before us, three large walls connect to a floor of carpet, with rows of books on each one. Then, in the center of the floor, a single wooden table with a dark green tablecloth laying on top of it appears.

On the table, books scatter about as a single metal chair appears behind the table, between it and the rows along the wall. I watch as the three figures walk over to the open room and start to examine the different books on the table.

"I think I am going to take a seat behind the table," Number Two says, making his way around the table. As we watch, he continues toward the chair and then pulls it out, its legs scraping across the floor. He then sits before pulling it back underneath the table. Once secure, we watch Number Two rummage through the various books before beginning to flip through the pages of one on his left.

"You should sign one of those books," Omrel speaks, causing Number Two to lift his head from out of the pages.

We then watch as a red pen appears within his hand and his eyes shift back to the blank page waiting for him on the table.

"Number Two, sign the book with red ink," the voice rings out from above everyone. As the others watch him sign on the page, I move a look a little to include Manuel as he continues to stare.

"What is this voice speaking?" I whisper, sending Manuel's gaze over to me.

"It's Number Three's narrator," Manuel replies.

My eyes go back to three men outside as they continue to watch as Number Two finishes up his signature.

"Number One then approaches the table and grabs the book to look at the page Number Two just signed," the narrator speaks once more.

We watch as Omrel turns around with the book in hand as he makes his way closer to the train. After stopping next to Number Three, Number Two remains alone behind the table, causing the others to look back at him.

"You should really come over here, Uno," Omrel says, catching the attention of Number Two as he clambers from the chair.

As the chair skids backward, the table shakes, causing the books to toss close to the edge. Omrel watches as Uno shoves his way around the table as he huffs and puffs toward the other two men. After taking a step, Uno stops and turns around as a pen glitters in the shining light from above. He makes his way over, leaning over as he grabs hold of the pen. Placing it inside his pocket, Uno looks over his shoulder at everyone.

"I want this pen," Uno replies.

Omrel and the other figure remain motionless, watching Uno make his way over to them as he stops on the opposite of Omrel. Arriving by their side, he turns his attention back to Manuel and me.

"The three wonder what choice Guillermo will make," the narrating voice says.

I look back to Manuel, who continues to smirk as he stares out the window. Before long, they shift their glance over to me as I stare back in confusion.

"What is it?" I ask, glancing back at the three figures outside.

"They are waiting for you to pick which one you prefer," Manuel replies, lifting his hand toward the window.

I turn toward the three figures as they stare back in silence and I scratch the side of my head. "Why me?"

"Simple, this is your story," Manuel replies.

"Okay, then I choose second person," I reply, watching as the light on both sides of Omrel lose their intensity. After shutting off, the two men disappear into the darkness, leaving Omrel alone.

"You won't regret this decision," Omrel replies, when suddenly the light above him disappears. As the darkness entangles its way throughout the last shreds of glare, his shadow dissipates into the emptiness.

I lean back and shift my attention back to Manuel in time to watch him shift in the chair. Before I can speak, a shadow catches my attention in the doorway, and I look up. The shadow creeps inside and bends along the curves of the wall, when suddenly the source appears. It is Omrel, carrying a slice of pizza as spots of grease stain his cheeks.

Omrel pauses in the doorway, shifting his attention back and forth from Manuel to me. Stretching wildly, I look at his chest, finding it to be free from anything other than a single splatter of tomato sauce. "Is class still in session?"

"Yep, just finished the Three Perspectives and now we are heading to the Wheel of Emotions," Manuel replies.

Omrel drops the pizza and it slams to the ground as he smiles before taking a seat next to Manuel. "Well then, let's get going, shall we?" He gets comfortable with his back up against the cushion.

"What is the Wheel of Emotions?" I ask, feeling the ground start to rumble and vibrate. The world outside begins to move as the train chugs along.

"It is where your friend is waiting for you," Manuel replies, shifting his attention to the world outside the window.

"Periwinkle?" I ask.

Manuel nods his head, causing me to shift my attention to the window where the darkness continues as the faint light dissipates. Growing darker with each second, the entire room remains quiet as we all wait for any sign of change. For a while nothing came as the darkness passes us by, until suddenly, lights sparkle from within its depths. Then, just as the lights brighten, waves of thunder take over the silence, louder than the clanging of the train tracks. The sound, becoming louder and louder, continues as the train gets closer and the darkness breaks apart before our eyes. Suddenly, between the rounds of sound, drums clang as we start to see the source of the noises.

"Welcome to the Wheel."

I look out the window to see us approach a massive wheel with various icons along the rim of it. Between each icon, golden pegs protrude from the lines as the Wheel gently spins around. Behind the Wheel, a section of audience cheers as the drumming ceases, leaving the only raucous applause. The lights we had struggled to see in the darkness are now brighter and bouncing all about, reflecting around the area. Before our eyes, more lights blast downward, revealing a figure standing upon a podium next to the Wheel. The figure faces the crowd before ripping off his hat, revealing a familiar style.

"PERIWINKLE!"

The cheering ceases and the his head bows to the ground as the hat drops to his side. He then slowly makes turns around, allowing us to see the front side of him. It was indeed Periwinkle, and as his eyes meet mine, he erupts in joy, tossing the hat high into the air. As the hat falls back down, the audience starts to cheer, the lights aiming at our cabin.

He then sits down onto the ledge of the platform and drops back down to the main level before he charges toward the train. After a couple of large steps, he comes to a halt near the side of the cabin. Because of the window separating us, Periwinkle leans in and places his hands on both sides of his face to block the glare from the lights. His eyes shift between the three of us before he pushes himself back and lifts up his bright coat. He reaches his hand into one of the pockets and pulls out a cane wrapped with bright red and blue stripes.

Periwinkle places the cane against the wall, tapping it on the surface before pulling it back to his side. The crowd goes quiet as we watch and debate on what is to come when suddenly the lights within the cabin darken. Once pitch black, the silence is broken by a single girlish scream echoing out from behind me.

I shift my glance, watching as Periwinkle fades from view and I search for Manuel and Omrel on the other side of the room. "What happened?"

The room replies with silence when suddenly the lights turn back on revealing Omrel crouching down in his seat. "I felt something touch me," Omrel mumbles, his face pale.

That's when it hits me, the seat next to Omrel is empty, and Manuel is nowhere to be found. I look above the seat and beneath the chairs, finding nothing not even a trace of where he had gone. Before I can continue my search, the walls of the cabin start to tremble as two separate bells ring inside. We watch as the wall falls to the ground, smashing the glass of the window against the ground.

I turn back to Omrel, who slumps back down into his seat, grabbing a hold of the seatbelt strap hanging off the side. He then tosses it over his body and locks it into place before looking back at me. I shift my attention to my seat, spotting a similar one over one of my arm rests. I grab a hold of it and toss it over, locking myself into the seat as well. I turn to watch as Periwinkle steps onto the wall and into the room.

Periwinkle makes his way over to Omrel first, and then makes his way back to me. After delivering a nod, he then walks to the space separating us from the flickering lights outside. He stops on the edge of the sloping cabin wall, his toes falling to a rest on the inside wall. He turns back when suddenly lights from all around ignite, revealing every last detail of the surrounding space.

The walls glisten from the reflections around us as row after row of random figures sit down upon their seat, providing an audience for this emotional game show. Their various faces change to happiness as the lights around the Wheel sparkle brightly and the ground starts to quake. Struggling to catch a glimpse, I watch as the ground between the backside of the Wheel and the audience spins open. Once it is open, a band appears in uniforms that perfectly match Periwinkle's. Holding their instruments to the side, one of the trumpeters steps forward before nodding his head. He then places the trumpet up to his mouth and begins to a play a solo chorus line before he stops. The trumpeter bows and then steps back into line as the audience all around roars to their feet.

"Ladies and Gentleman of the audience!" Periwinkle yells as his voice echoes all over the room, "The time has come to find the next participant on Guillermo's Emotion Wheel!"

As his words escape, the bright lights dim, sending the entire room back into the darkness. Before I can speak, projection lights fly across the room, causing different sections to light up. Spinning around the room, my eyes catch a glimpse of Periwinkle as his feet cause the wall to bend and creak. Just as he disappears into the darkness, the beam spins into the cabin and into our eyes, blinding me momentarily as it moves on to the next section. I struggle to open my eyes wide as tears drip down the sides of my face.

"Are you crying?" Omrel whispers from the darkness.

"I can't see anything beyond the blurriness," I reply, struggling to shake off the specks of glitter blocking my vision. After a couple moments, my vision finally returns as I am able to make out the solid beams of light that continue to spin around the room.

I then catch sight of one beam as it approaches the area next to us and I shut my eyes quickly. The light approaches and covers up the darkness before it suddenly stops. Turning my head to the side, I open the eye away from the light and look over at Omrel to see him staring back at me. Before I can say anything, the audience starts to cheer and the band plays as the light remains still. Then suddenly a finger snap sends all the noise into silence and another light onto the podium next to the giant wheel.

Standing in the center, Periwinkle strikes a showman's pose, with his hand high into the air. I watch as Periwinkle lowers his arm and then looks over to the audience as they remain silent. "The light has chosen."

I watch as Periwinkle turns around and looks me in the eyes as the crowd goes wild at the sound of his voice.

"What is he talking about?" Omrel's voice faintly breaks from the loud roars.

"You have been chosen," a familiar voice sounds.

Before I can discover the source, a bit of pressure squeezes my shoulder, causing me to turn around. My eyes find Manuel removing his hand as he steps around both of us into the darkness. As he continues forward, I free myself from the chair and look over at Omrel, who remains seated in his own chair. "Are you coming?"

"Nope, this is your story," Omrel replies, lifting his hand and pointing in the Wheel's direction.

"What do you mean my story?" I ask.

"This has always been about what you wanted to write about," Manuel replies, causing me to look back to him.

I then watch him step back into the darkness as the dimming light behind me intensifies, blinding the entire room. Struggling to find Manuel, I listen as the roars of the crowd fade away as the drumming band ceases.

"Please welcome our next contestant … GUILLERMO!" Periwinkle's voice echoes, sending the audience back into a frenzy. Once his voice fades to a whisper behind the curtain of roaring, the band starts to play and the drums take the lead. Timing it perfectly, I turn about to face them between the beats of the drum.

The Next Contestant

As I make my way forward, the light dims to allow me to see the room as the crowd erupts with applause. I then see Periwinkle on top of his platform as he lifts his arm into the air. My eyes shift when suddenly the dim light moves downward and brightens on top of a platform walkway between us. With a deep breath, I take one step onto the cabin wall and continue down toward the first part of the platform as it sits on the ground. Getting closer, the beam shifts down the walkway, revealing its entirety to me as I stop just shy of the first step. Before I can lift my foot, the first piece shifts its color from silver to red.

Icarefully lift my foot and gently place it onto the red surface as my other foot follows suit. Just before I take another step, the red gives way to green and the next piece turns red. Once more, I take a step onto it with it turning color as I continue to keep my eyes on the ground ahead of me. The cycle of color change continues until finally I arrive at the final piece in the shadow of Periwinkle's platform. The crowd goes silent as I look up at Periwinkle, who looks over at a stand between himself and the massive wheel.

Periwinkle then leans over and extends a hand, which I grasp as he gives me a boost upwards and onto the stand. Once steady on my feet, I watch as Periwinkle motions his arm to point over to the far end of the platform.

Looking over, my eyes gaze upon a silver and gold mechanism

with a single green lever directly in the center. However, just as I attempt to take a step, another light overhead shines, revealing the massive wheel and all of its panels.

"Please observe your emotional options," Periwinkle replies, keeping the audience around us silent.

My eyes inspect the different panels of the wheel as I discover the various emotions represented. Starting at the very top was a human face with a toothy smile, while on the other end is a face with frown face. Between them, a face with a mouth that appears to be neutral, despitea single tear on its cheek.

Noticing every emotional tile, my eyes catch a glimpse of one that is different from the rest. Sparkly and glittery, this one carries no emotion, just the word EPIC. As my brain starts to wonder about what it does, I shift my attention to Periwinkle to see him pandering to the crowd. Catching sight of me, I listen as the crowd silences, causing Periwinkle to turn around.

"Any final questions?" Periwinkle asks, placing his hands down onto his cane as it stands on the ground.

"Actually, I have one," I reply, pointing upwards to the EPIC panel. I watch as Periwinkle's eyes follow my arm upwards and I can see the reflective shimmer in his eyes.

"That is the EPIC Tile, few have gotten it to land on that one," Periwinkle says, his eyes looking back down on me.

I momentarily look over at the tile once more before shifting my attention to the lever in front of me. With a deep breath, I step toward it, hearing the crowd start to cheer and chant. I had never heard Guillermo's name said so loudly; it's even louder than the sounds of the trumpets from the band. My hand shakes as I reach for the lever, and I can feel the bead of sweat sliding down my forehead. Struggling to keep my eyes from looking elsewhere, I trap the lever in the palm of my hand. As my grip strengthens, the band quiets except for the steady line of beats from the drummers to keep the tension going in the room. Then, with a mighty gulp, the muscles in my arm tighten and my arm drops down, pulling the lever with it.

As I feel the spring stretch, I release my hold, hearing the mechanical grinding of the wheel next to me. Looking over, the wheel starts to spin faster as each panel catches on a single blue arrow. It hits each peg, but the wheel continues around as the colors begin to blend into each other, even the glittery surface of the epic one. That's when the crowd cheers widly as I turn to Periwinkle when he places a hand onto his hat to keep it on his head. His eyes spin in circles as he struggles to keep track of the tiles. That's when the crowd's cheers turn into a gasp, causing me to turn to the wheel.

It begins to slow down, revealing the individual panels as they spin around, the clanging of the pegs hitting the arrow filling the air. The pace of strikes lessens as my eyes catch sight of the different panels and the crowd *oohs* and *ahhs* at the possibilities. It continues to slow as the stopper's effect takes hold, the panels slowly passing the arrow.

That's when it happened: the spinning stopped and the audience falls silent along with the beating drums. I struggle to figure out what it means as I hear something slam down onto the floor at my feet. I look over just in time to see Periwinkle rushing over to me with a rosy grin from ear to ear.

"You did it!" Periwinkle screams over the crowd.

Then, just as I attempt to get a reply in, fireworks explode from behind the bleachers and burst above the grounds. I can't keep track of everything as I realize I haven't looked at the wheel. As my eyes drift over, the room goes silent and I see the arrow nestled between the golden rungs of the EPIC panel. I watch as the other emotions disappear, leaving me to digest the results of my spin.

As I stand back in awe, a shadow creeps into my view as Periwinkle makes his way toward the wheel. I watch as the platform lifts up and moves him closer to the top. Once he was at equal height, Periwinkle leans over and grabs the panel before pulling it off the wheel. With it now in hand, he throws it into the air among the exploding lights as I look on.

I watch as it explodes into various bundles of lights that form various emotions. As my eyes blur with the onslaught of the bright lights, I turn back to Periwinkle as he pumps his fists up and down. "What did I do?"

The audience quiets just as the final firework explodes in the air. Periwinkle, meanwhile, looks down at me, his smirk glued on his face. "You have gotten the EPIC emotion!"

"Which means what for the next story?" I ask back, watching his smile shrink down.

"It means that, rather than just a singular emotion guiding your story, you are going to have multiple ones," another voice blurts out. I turn to see Omrel standing a few feet from me.

"Thus making it an epic novel, filled with twists and turns," Periwinkle adds.

My eyes shift back to him as I hear Omrel making his way to my side. His steps stop as I keep my eyes on Periwinkle. Suddenly, the lights above our heads start to flicker as the ground quakes. Struggling to keep my balance, I look up at the lights as they sway back and forth until they finally go out. As the darkness surrounds us, the dim lights from the cabin allow me to see Periwinkle and Omrel.

All the sounds that had filled the room were gone, not even a whisper. I look over Periwinkle's shoulder to see nothing, just open space as everything had gone without a trace.

"What are you looking for?" Periwinkle asks, looking over his shoulder as well.

"The wheel … the band … the audience … they are all gone," I reply, once more glancing out into the darkness.

"All gone since the game is over," Omrel replies, taking another step forward.

"Where do they go?" I ask, turning my attention to him as Periwinkle takes a couple of steps closer to us.

"Back into position for when Guillermo wants to create another story," Periwinkle replies.

"What about you?" I ask.

"Well, I return to the Imagination Circus to give the idea a test run," Periwinkle replies, placing his hat back on his head.

Before I can say anything, the train's horn blares from behind us and we look back as steam creeps from out of the bottom.

"Please board for the finale," Manuel says, peeking his head from out of the cabin.

I watch as Omrel and Periwinkle make their way toward the train as I remain still. They take a couple more steps before looking back at me as I struggle to lift my feet.

"You coming?" they ask.

After nodding my head, I make my way forward, passing them by as they continue behind me. "Wait, what is in the finale?"

Moving forward, Periwinkle looks at me as I see Omrel keeping his focus on the opening.

"You didn't think we were going to let you miss the finale to that fight in the arena, did you?" Periwinkle answers, turning his attention back to the cabin.

The light starts to take over, keeping the darkness at bay as Manuel stands in the center. Getting closer, he moves out of the way and we step from the end of the fallen wall. I watch as both Omrel and Periwinkle make their way inside, sitting down in their seats. Manuel looks back at me as my eyes drop down to the inclining floor.

"You coming?" Manuel asks.

Remaining silent, I take a deep breath and step onto the wall as it gives a little. After a few more steps, I find myself standing on the edge of the darkness. I place my hand against the frame, taking a step inside, feeling them staring. Trying to ignore them, I take a seat across the cabin before seeing Manuel staring at me from the cabin's entrance. "So when do we get moving?"

Manuel turns to Omrel and Periwinkle who both look at the open doorway before turning back to him. He then looks back at the wall as it lifts upwards and back into place. As the steam rushes past the cabin, it seals shut and they turn back to me. Without a word, all three point a finger out into the darkness of the entrance.

"Out and make a right," Omrel says as the ground shivers and the train speeds up.

"Look for a door the same color as my name," Periwinkle replies.

I nod my head with their guidance and push myself back to a standing position. With a wave of my hand, I make my way outside into the hallway before turning to the right. The hall fades into the darkness beyond the cabin's light, revealing nothing. Then, with a deep breath, I make my way into it, keeping my eyes peeled for this periwinkle-colored door. Step after step, it was all the same, sinking darkness which faintly reveals open windows to the left. Across from them, a bland gray wall with rivets spread throughout, bouncing with every tiny bump.

"This will help," Omrel's voice echoes, causing me to look back.

Before I can turn around, I spot something bounce along the floor and smack into the side of my leg. As it drops in a heap, I kneel down to retrieve it. I lift it into my hand, seeing that it's a miniature brain, divided into sections. The light turns solid, reflecting off of the surfaces around me, guiding my way into the darkness. "Thank you."

"You're welcome," Omrel replies before his shadow disappears into the room.

My attention shifts back to the hall, watching as the darkness retreats and the light carves a guiding path. Continuing my trek, I look all over for the door, when my eyes shift momentarily to an open window nearby. Twinkly darkness passes by as the train speeds along the flickering tracks.

Shaking my head, I turn back and continue my journey. The wall to my right remains doorless until something near the end of the glow catches my eye. It was a tiny sparkle before it disappeared and I froze in my tracks. I looked down at the brain light, warming my hand, and then turned back to the end of the hall. I threw my arm forward then and released the brain, sending it flying down the hall.

Section by section, it reveals the boring yet repetitive areas in front of me before it settles down by where I thought the tiny speck was located. That's when it revealed something, a bluish door, sparkling with the reflections of the light bouncing off of it. My eyes widen as I take off, making my closer to it. My eyes focus on the door as my feet come to a halt just shy of it.

The door was indeed periwinkle from top to bottom, a doormat camoflauging itself along the gray floor in front of the door. "Turn the knob," I said to myself.

I look up at the bronze doorknob sitting by itself and reach for it. I turn it counter-clockwise as it unlocks, and pops the door open from its frame. I throw the door open, only to find myself face-to-face with an empty room. However, looking again, my eyes catch sight of a massive curtain,a dark red in color. In the corner of the curtain, a golden rope hangs down from the roof. Next to it, a white board sits on the wall with words faintly written on its surface.

Making my way closer, the words begin to take shape Mere steps away, my mind finally puts the scrambled writing together to form the words, "Pull the rope for the finale." My eyes then shift to the rope as it sways with the bouncing of the train. Looking down at my hand, I move it upward and wrap it around the golden strands before pulling it downward. Releasing my hold, it shoots upward and out of view and suddenly the room starts to shake violently. Tossing me back and forth, it stops as the curtain starts to flap around and roll into itself. Continuing upwards, the curtain disappears, revealing a darkness that not even the light can break through.

Looking around in the silence, lights begin to appear from the roof, around a sign as it drops down into view. Illuminating gigantic letters, my eyes once again make out the word on the sign. It says, "Sit down for the finale." Turning my attention to the room, I jump back as I spot a brown loveseat next to me. Confused about how it got there, I glance around to see what else is in the room.

"Please take a seat," a voice says aloud.

My eyes dart across the roof as my hand feels for the armrest of the loveseat nearby. Feeling its plushy texture, I step around the front of it as my eyes continue to search for the source of the voice. Sitting down, the chair bends slightly to mold around me as I place my back up against the pillowy seat. Once I was comfortable, I look around the room once more.

"Are you ready?" the voice says.

Once more, my eyes dart across the sky, finding nothing but more darkness. "Maybe, but who are you?"

"I am one of the voices inside Guillermo's mind, kinda like you—except I have no form," the voice replies as suddenly a light appears in the center of the darkness.

Then, before I can attempt to get up from my seat, something straps me down across my legs and I feel the chair start to move. Going forward into the light, I see an opening just large enough for the chair as it heads right toward it. As the loveseat speeds through the hole, I see it before my eyes, the arena stage completely set from where the last scene finished: the two fighters standing along a sandy floor with a raucous crowd cheering all around.

Gray walls wrap around the two men as the sun blazes down from above. Both men, sweating and out of breath, stare at each other with their weapons in attack position. Even as blood drips from cuts along their frames, the two men struggle to find an opening.

The attacker makes the first move as he swings his sword in the man's direction. He dodges the blow by striking it with his mace, which causes both weapons to shatter in their hands. Leaving nothing but handles, the remains of the weapons sprinkle across the ground. The attacker looks down at the jagged leftover before turning his attention to the man as he stares at the splintered wood left from the mace.

He then drops the handle onto the ground and charges at the man, sending him back on his heels. Unable to defend himself from the attacker, the man is slammed to the ground. As he slams his fists into the attacker's back, he slams him into the sand, sending out a shockwave in all directions. The attacker chuckles as he circles the man, who struggles to regain his breath before kneeling down next to him. He wraps his hand around the man's throat, causing him to try to pry his fingers off.

The attacker then lifts him off the ground, and slams his feet before pushing him backward. As the man stumbles, the attacker unleashes a flurry of blows against the man's body, which sends him crumbling to a knee. The man spits up a glob of blood as he rubs his hands on the forming bruises beneath his skin. His watery eyes rise from the grains of sand and look toward the attacker, who flexes his muscles.

The man slams his hand into the ground, bracing himself to get back to his feet. His chest expands with every breath as the man stares at the attacker when he taunts the man by pandering to the crowd. The cheers turn to boos as the attacker points to the man who slowly lifts his hands.

"You're done!" the attacker screams.

He charges at the man who sinks down to kneel. Then, just as the attacker tries to grab hold, the man slides to the side and watches as the attacker stumbles into the sand. Listening to the crowd as the tide turns, the man charges forward and jumps into the air. Reaching his fist back, he falls onto the attacker as he throws his hand forward. He watches as it connects with the attackers back, sending the attacker flat onto the sand. Then, after delivering a few more punches to various parts of his back, the man gets back up and then hits the attacker in the ribs with a stiff kick. Taking a step back, the man watches as the attacker groans as he lifts his face from out of the sand. Staring at him through a facefull of sand, the attacker rises to his feet, throwing sand furiously in each direction.

"Come get me," the man replies, placing his fists in front of his body.

The attacker spits blood to the side before charging at the man with hands swinging violently. Before any hits land, the man steps off to the side, tripping the man as he stumbles back into the sand. The attacker punches the sand in frustration, turning his attention back to the man whose breath calms.

I then watch the attacker charging at the man once again. Just as he attempts a barbaric swing, the man moves out of the way, causing the attacker to nearly fall again. Except this time, the attacker swings his other arm and throws sand into the man's eyes. Blinded, the man struggles to clear his sight as the attacker sneaks behind him. Then the attacker grabs hold of the man's neck and his lower back. He moves him forward as the man attempts to reach back to grab the attacker's arms, but the attacker carries the struggling man over to the far end of the area. Just as he gets near the end of the area, the attacker throws the man out of my view with the crowd booing.

Watching on, the attacker screams before stepping out, and I feel the seat start to move, following the fighters to the left. In front of me, a continuation of the battle appears, except it had spilled outside.

The brutish attacker stands above the smaller man as among fallen rubble, a large rock in his hands. He reaches back and turns to the man with it held high. As he makes moves forward, the man shifts to his back and tries to scurry away from the attacker. Before he can get any farther, the attacker grips the brick with both hands and slams it down to man's chest. Just before it hits, the man catches it, freezing it inbetween them. Before anything else happens, the scene fades to black and my eyes widen in shock.

"Sorry, it appears we are searching the cranium for the ending of the finale," the voice echoes out.

My attention shifts elsewhere as sounds of rummaging and crashing come through the silence when the motion stops. "What is going on?"

"Oh sorry, it appears we have located the final scene," the voice replies.

Suddenly, the darkness opens up, revealing a cliff in front of a mountain chain as trees bend in the wind. There is no sign of the fighters or the sandy ground or even the roaring crowd, just the tranquil scene in front of me. After waiting a few moments for the fighters to appear, my eyes wander about as the only sounds continue to be the whistling winds. "What happened next?"

This time the voice doesn't answer back. Instead, from the right of the screen a familiar figure appears behind the helm of a wheelbarrow. Inside, a three-dimensional representation of the words *like*, *as*, and *was* bounce all about. The figure then stops and places the wheelbarrow at the edge of the cliff as he turns to me. "Periwinkle?"

"Hey, what are you doing here?" Periwinkle replies, walking around the backside of the wheelbarrow.

"Waiting for the final scene," I reply, watching as Periwinkle leans over and picks up the word *was* from out of the rest.

"That voice didn't tell you?" Periwinkle replies, tossing the word over the cliff.

"Tell me what?" I ask, watching Periwinkle once again making his way over to the wheelbarrow.

"The finale ends in a cliffhanger like this one," Periwinkle replies, grabbing hold of another word and throwing it over the cliff.

"What is a cliffhanger?" I ask.

The next thing I know the scene goes black as tiny lights on the ceiling flicker on. Once the light steadies, I look around the room, finding a shadow creeping along the floorboards. Periwinkle steps out of the shadows and into the light with his usual grin on his face.

Reaching the End

" *That* is a cliffhanger," Periwinkle replies. As he finishes his statement, the belt across me loosens up, allowing me to get up from the seat.

"I still don't get it," I say, scratching the side of my face.

"The point of cliffhangers is to leave you guessing," Periwinkle replies, looking over at the seat behind me.

"True, but isn't it good to give the reader an ending?" I say, watching as Periwinkle makes his way behind the chair.

"Not in some cases, but, anyways, it's time to move on to our next step in the storyline," Periwinkle replies as he taps the top of the seat.

My gaze shifts over, watching as the seat sends glittering lights down to its feet. It then flutters outward, and onto the wooden panels before dying out. I hesistanly make my over to the chair and I turn my back to it. Reaching back, I place my hands on each of the armrests. My eyes shut as I sink down into the chair behind me. Once I meet the cushion, my eyes reopen to find myself back inside the cabin of the train along with the others. Looking over at me, Periwinkle smirks as I look around the room to find everything as it was.

"I'm guessing you found the cliffhanger," Manuel says with a smirk.

My head nods as my stomach tumbles over itself with nausea as the others lean back into their chairs. "Sorry, just a lot of twists and turns."

"Yeah, the finale will do that to you," Periwinkle replies.

"So what have you learned about writing a story?" Omrel asks, watching as Manuel and Periwinkle look over at him.

They then turn their attention to me as my hand leaves my stomach and touches my chin. As my thumb presses one side and another finger rubs the other, my eyes survey them as my mind thinks up an answer. "It begins with a basis of characters, setting, and theme."

"Okay, what next?" Periwinkle asks.

"Using personal inspiration and focus, you create events that, at the end, will build your character upward," I reply.

"Sometimes downward, or both," Manuel adds.

"Yes and then what else?" Periwinkle asks.

"The ending can be a cliffhanger or something certain," I reply.

Without a word, I look over when something catches the corner of my eye. Steam rises over the glass of the window as the train unleashes a piercing screech, echoing outside. The train slows down, which causes the floor beneath our feet to vibrate, until the train comes to a stop. We all got up at once and make our way out into the hallway. The lights overhead turn on, revealing the cream-colored walls surrounding us. A red stripe zigzags from one side to the other, turning my attention back to the direction in front of us. In the distance, a double door sits in the center of the wall, the red traveling around its frame.

Before I can even take a step, the door splits open, allowing some of the remnants of steam inside the hallway. In single file, we make our way toward the door as it locks in place, allowing the pulsating lights outside to enter inside. Once we reach the doorway, I watch Omrel step out of the train and onto the floor beyond, followed by Periwinkle. As he places his hat on his head, I step off the ledge and join them before turning back. Still inside, Manuel places his hand on the frame as the train's horn rings out and the steam grows in strength. He looks over to the front, and then turns to us as we stand in silence.

"Are you coming or staying?" Periwinkle asks, causing me to shift my glance from him back to Manuel.

Before he can say anything, the train roars once more as we watch

Manuel nod his head. "Someone has to guide this train of thought down these guiding tracks," he replies.

I turn my head to Omrel and Periwinkle, watching them nod their heads as I look back to Manuel, seeing him lift his hand into the air, waving it back and forth. The doors unlock from their position as he removes his other hand from the frame. Then, the doors slide shut and lock before the train unleashes another blaring horn. The train's wheels begin to spin as it moves forward along the tracks. Gaining speed, we watch as it chugs away and speeds off into a tunnel as lights fluctuate around the entrance. As the remaining steam sinks down to the ground, I look over to Periwinkle and Omrel as they turn around. I turn as well, finding myself face-to-face with the three circus rings where I had first encountered Periwinkle.

I watch as the two of them continue toward the rings and I stand back in the distance. Taking a couple of more steps they stop in place, looking back at me as I make my way forward.

"Why the hesitation?" Periwinkle asks.

"I can feel Guillermo beginning to come up with a new idea," I reply, looking around the room as exploding lights erupt throughout the room.

"We know," Omrel says, watching the lights as they continue to explode around us.

"Yep this one is about a bear and … bobcat," Periwinkle replies.

"How do you know?" I ask, taking a couple of steps closer.

"We are part of the same imaginative world," Periwinkle replies.

"I mean, we are figments just like you," Omrel adds.

"Besides just look at the roof," Periwinkle says, causing me to turn towards him.

I look over when he points upwards to the roof where the flashing lights seem to be avoiding. From out of the darkness in the ceiling, an image of a bear similar to the one we had seen in the classroom moves back and forth. Another image of a bobcat pops out to his side and appears to turn its head toward the other image. We watch as, beneath their feet, a thin layer of grass appears and a cascading sky above them. Meanwhile, trees and brush grow from out of nowhere to set the stage. Then, just as I start to wait for the next thing, the two animals walk along the grass. Heading into the background, the scenery turns to an ocean environment with a palm tree near the coast. As they disappear into the sea, the images disappear into the darkness as the exploding lights cease.

My attention turns to Periwinkle as he wipes a tear from his eyes before he turns to Omrel who lets out a deep breath.

"What is it?" Periwinkle asks.

Saying nothing, I watch Omrel exit the center of my vision and head off toward one of the walls of the room. I turn to watch as he starts to make his way over to the opposite end of the room. Waiting for him, a fluffy brown chair sits on top of the floor as the light dims when Omrel steps in front of it. He turns about and gently sits on the bottom cushion, falling flush with the comfort of the chair.

"I am going to another section to help distribute the brain power," Omrel replies, sitting back into the chair before vanishing from our view.

Continuing to stare after him, I look to Periwinkle. "What just happened?" I ask, watching Periwinke brush himself off as he proceeds over to the final ring at the far end.

"He must return to provide guidance for any lost trains of thought," Periwinkle replies, taking another step.

"I guess every thought needs a conductor," I reply, watching Periwinkle getting closer to the opening. Once he steps through, Periwinkle turns back as I start to make my way over to him. However, before I can make it any further footsteps start to echo throughout the room. Turning back, I begin to see the outline of a figure making its way rapidly toward us.

"Hold on a second," the voice replies.

Struggling to make out the figure, it comes into view, revealing the exhausted form of the teacher from the classroom. We pause as he continues into the lights of the lines of thought. After wiping his face of the few beads of sweat, the teacher comes to a stop just steps in front of both of us.

"What is it?" Perwinkle asks, his eyes shifting between the final door and the teacher struggling to regain his composure.

"Before you enter the conclusion of our story tour, I want to show you the Central Center of Ideas," replies the teacher, pointing over to an area of the room darker than the rest. Before either of us can speak, a light over head of the area begins to flicker, steadily revealing a single metal door along the wall. Along its body, the words *inner thoughts* are written inside a bluish gray background.

"What is the Central Center of Ideas?" Periwinkle asks, watching as the teacher gingerly makes his way over to the faintly lit door.

"It's where Guillermo goes to in order to search for brand new ideas for his stories," I reply with no hesitation, causing the teacher to stop in his tracks.

He looks back, just on the verge of the realm of light, as I first look at Periwinkle and then at him. His stare was a mix of wonder and disbelief as I stared blankly, wondering what I had said that had caused his surprise. "How did you know that?"

"I heard Guillermo mentioning something about tapping into his inner thoughts," I reply cautiously.

"Why did I not know that? After all, I'm the ringmaster of his thoughts," Periwinkle whispers, causing me to shift my attention.

"It was only a one-time thing, about the time he finished the book about angels and demons," I reply, watching as Periwinkle's face drops a bit.

"Either way, come on," the teacher replies, shifting my attention to him, finding him to be within feet of the shining door. He reaches his hand out and places it around the handle before twisting it. With a single pull, the door creaks and swings open, allowing us to see the dark room that stands on the other side. He then motions us forward, watching as we come closer.

We arrive at the door, only to watch as the teacher makes his way inside. Disappearing within the shadows, we watch as the darkness swallows him up whole. I then turn to Periwinkle, who starts to make his way into the doorway before being taken by the darkness. Before I can join them, the lights start to brighten, allowing me to see the insides of the room.

Within, I find rows and rows of metal storage shelves without a single thing upon them, as far as the eye can see. Then from the corner of my eye, Periwinkle takes a couple steps toward one of the rows. Once in the room, an annoying vaccumning sound starts, forcing my eyes upwards. My eyes catch sight of a series of vents blowing into the room before quickly stopping and then closing shut. As the sound evaporates into silence, my eyes begin to take in the remainder of the room. Everything is clean, from the metallic frameworks of the storage to the air inside, without a single speck of dust.

The sound of footsteps beats into the room, forcing my eyes around the room, looking for the source. That's when I found it: two shadows making their way toward one of the bare storages toward the left. "Periwinkle, is that you?"

Hearing no response, I charge forward to the open hall as the shadows disappear into the blinking lights. A chuckle echoes about the room, and my head jerks left and then right in search of the sound, before another round of laughter forces my head back to the left. Without hesitation, I turn the corner, finding myself between two rows of open space. That's when my eyes catch sight of a single cardboard box, sitting on the center shelf. Beneath it, redish liquid flows from the box's corner and makes its way to the edge of the shelving. It then slides of the edge and cascades onto the dark tile floor.

"What is that?" I whisper, gulping as my feet lift off the ground.

With each passing step, a putrid smell fills my nostrils, causing me to pause as I feel sick. Struggling to ignore the nauseating smell, I spot a single word smeared on the sides of the box. However before I can read it, the box begins to jiggle, forcing me to reach out and grab hold of it. As the puddling liquid streams between the cracks in my fingers, a cold chill shoots down my spine. My hands rise, with box in my grasp, as the liquid continues to drizzle downward into a swelling puddle at my feet. The bubbling fluid spreads about until suddenly the liquid weakens at the source. My heart stops as I place the box down in the center of the red patch as my eyes look for a crease or fold. That's when I spot a cut along the far edge of the box, focusing my attention upon it. However, just as I go to reach for it, two shadows extend onto the wall directly ahead of me.

"What you got there?" a familiar voice asks.

My head turns to see the faces of Mozen and Periwinkle as they steadily make their way over to me. They hasten their pace until finally they stop at the edge of the liquid before it can touch their bare feet.

"What are you doing with that box?" Mozen asks, looking all

about at the diminishing liquid.

"I was going to open it," I reply swiftly, turning my attention back to the box.

"Don't you know what is inside there?" Mozen grumbles, taking a step forward, crushing the liquid into the solid floor. He then took another step forward before kneeling at my side, pointing his nail at the single word written along the sides.

"Think," Periwinkle says, reading the word written in red smear.

"Do you know what is inside there?" I ask, struggling to keep my hands from reaching for the cover.

"Let me show you," Mozen replies, causing me to pause as he reaches for the tiny cut along the edge. As his hands touch the box, the liquid evaporates. Before I can attempt to take a deep breath, Mozen rips open the cover, revealing the innards of the box to me.

Before my eyes, an emptiness sits at the bottomg of this cardboard container, away from the light trying to intrude inside. Unable to see much, I perch my hands along the brim of the sides in order to try to get a better look. Still, I see nothing, which causes me to look up at Mozen as he curves his head around my own so he can see the box on the other end. "What is in here?"

Mozen shifts his attention to me when he reaches down into the darkness, sending my eyes along with his hands. Suddenly, sounds of rumaging and crumpling ring out from the space, which causes me to wonder what is within the darkness out of my sight.

I then watch as he pulls his hand back up with a stack of papers sitting on top of them. On top of each one were lines of writing, in a language I knew nothing about. However, Mozen's stare upon them forces me to try to decipher what exactly was on them.

"Remember the pages I threw down the drain?" Mozen says, turning his focus onto me.

My thoughts float back to our journey through the hallway where we first found him and that book, claiming it was the first story written by Guillermo. My gaze is then broken by him dropping the papers back into the darkness as his eyes become glassy as he continues to stare into the box.

"Everything ok?" Periwinkle asks, sending my attention over to him just momentarily.

"Something is not right," Mozen replies, lifting his head from out of the box as he begins to look all around the room.

"What is it?" I ask, watching as he then starts to examine the space above, when suddenly he stops cold. Before I can even turn, he points his finger up toward the roof, causing me to look.

"I found out where the majority of the ideas I ripped out went," Mozen replies.

That is when I saw what had caught Mozen's attention and is now holding mine along with it. In front of our eyes, around one of the vent vaccumns, is a layer of papers of a similar material as the ones he had just pulled from the bottom of the box. I watch as the papers completely jam up the inside, unleashing a horrific grinding noise. As the sound ceases, a grayish smoke appears from between the cracks of the papers as it climbs along the roof.

"That's isn't good," Periwinkle says.

Continuing to watch the vaccumn, the smoke builds and suddenly a faint orange glow starts to appear from out of the billowing smoke. I watch as shreds of burning paper start to drip down as I shift my attention to the others as they continue to look with concern. Their faces getting paler by the second, they gingerly turn away as a bubble of flames erupts outward. After stepping back, Mozen grabs hold of the box, causing me to turn our attention to him as beads of sweat slide down his forehead.

"What should we do?" I ask, watching as his eyes dart around. Before he can answer, an explosion of flames mushrooms downward, causing the papers to twirl about. The papers then return to their state as the flames calm even as the smoke continues to darken the room.

"Run away," Mozen replies, scurrying toward the opening at the far end of the aisle.

Periwinkle follows in his footsteps and I watch as a buzzing sound starts from above. My eyes catch sight of the vent as the paper starts to bend inwards, the sound getting louder. Then, as I catch sight of a tiny spark, I take off hot on Periwinkle's heels.

My eyes zero in on the corner, where I see both Mozen and Periwinkle ducking behind one of the storage posts. However, just before I can get to them, a loud explosion sends the paper flying over my head. The wave of air sends me flying toward them as they remain frozen in their hiding place. My eyes quickly shut as I fall within feet of Mozen, Periwinkle looking on helplessly. That's when I felt a massive pain shooting all over my body before it stops as the warmth takes over. My ears continue to ring, struggling to hear anything beyond a jumble of voices.

Feeling myself spinning out of control, my eyes reopen watching things return to normal. I see Periwinkle and Mozen turn to me as they open their mouths in the attempt to say something to me. Hearing nothing they were saying, my eyes drift upwards as I find myself in front of a cracking wall with papers stuck to it. As the buzzing sound silences, I look at my hands, which are trembling, pressed against the floor between piles of book pages.

"Hey, are you okay?" Periwinkle says, breaking through the shambles of my hearing.

Turning my attention to him, I see his look of concern as Mozen continues to look around the room. Then, before long, his head stops and he rushes over to the end of the aisle where they were hiding. I watch as Periwinkle charges over to me as Mozen reaches underneath the bottom row of shelving.

"Just shaken up," I reply, struggling to get to my feet. Periwinkle lifts my arm and places it over his shoulders to assist me to my feet. Once there, my eyes look over at Mozen as he pulls out the red box and examines it for damage.

"Yeah, sometimes if thoughts get backed up, they can explode," Periwinkle replies.

Meanwhile, my eyes lock onto Mozen, who shifts his attention from the box to me. He smirks as he moves the box to his side before making his way to us.

"Glad you're safe," Mozen says.

"Why is that box so important to you?" I ask, causing Mozen to stop in his tracks.

"It's the box that holds the journey of my friends," Mozen replies, opening up the lid.

Periwinkle and I then watch as he reaches inside, pulling out yellowish papes with lines of writing in all direction. He then brings them closer to his face before dropping them back down into the box.

"Mozen hopes that one day Guillermo will save the story and finally finish it," Periwinkle says.

Feeling strength return to my feet, I lift my arm off of Periwinkle, and test my balance. "Why hasn't he finished it?"

"Complications," Mozen says.

"Well Mozen, I hope Guillermo finishes it," I say, flexing my toes and fingers.

"Me too," Mozen replies. I watch Mozen as he looks back at the box before gently placing it on the shelf above where he had found it hidden. Once it was on the shelf, Mozen carefully removes his hands from the box and then turns his attention to us.

"Well, we best be getting out of here, before another explosion," Periwinkle says, causing me to gaze over at him.

I find him standing in front of the wall that had cracked after I crashed into it. He examines the wall and pulls out his cane from within his jacket. Periwinkle places the edge of it up against the wall and looks over to us. We watch as he taps it, causing the wall to tremble before crumbling down to the ground. Once the debris is clear, my eyes catch sight of the three rings in the distance as Periwinkle makes his way into the darker space. He then turns back to watch as I remain still.

"Where are we going?" I ask, watching as he stops after another step.

"To the final ring," Periwinkle replies. Suddenly the lights above the first two rings fade into darkness as the one above the other grows brighter.

"What is there?" I reply, peeking over his shoulder to see the average door sitting in the center of the red ring.

"Sacrifice and Success," Periwinkle replies.

Intrigued, my feet move me forward as I pass through the hole into the darkness along with Periwinkle. After getting even with Periwinkle, I look back to see Mozen remaining near the box. His back resting against the metallic frame of the shelf, he turns to us as we look back in silence. "Are you coming with us?"

I watch as he momentarily looks over at the box before looking back over at us.

"No I want to watch over the box until the day their adventure sees daylight," Mozen replies.

"How do you know that will happen?" I ask.

"Guillermo never lets an idea sit by itself," Periwinkle replies.

"Yep, and as you can see there is nothing else here," Mozen says, looking all around the room.

"Well then, I guess this is goodbye," I reply, turning my attention to Periwinkle who begins to walk toward the final ring.

"Maybe you'll see me again in one of his stories," Mozen replies, resting his head up against the metal between shelves.

I nod my head as I turn around before making my way in Periwinkle's footsteps. Heading to the ring, the light from the room darkens as the ones around the ring continue to brighten. Flashing, the lights bring us in closer as we pass through the opening in the barrier without a second glance. Our eyes lock onto the wooden door in front of us and Periwinkle arrives first as I slow down. He reaches for the doorknob and then stops himself from opening it. He then turns to me as I continue to stare at his hand. "What is it?"

"This is the final step," Periwinkle replies.

"What do you mean?" I reply.

Without an answer, I watch as Periwinkle twists the knob and pops open the door. As he swings the door open, my eyes widen as I catch sight of what is behind the door. It was another door, similar to the one that Periwinkle just opened, except surrounding this one is a bright light trying to get free. Squeezing out from all angles, the light brightens as Periwinkle steps off to the side of the doorway.

"This is where I leave you," Periwinkle says, motioning his hand over to the door.

"Where will you go?" I ask, approaching the door as Periwinkle watches on.

"I will be here, trying to control the hyperness of any thoughts that don't have a story," Periwinkle replies. I then watch as, with a grin on his face, he places his bright tophat back on top of his head. With it snug around his hair, Periwinkle steps back as I approach the doorway.

Not giving his words a second thought, my eyes lock around the doorknob as my hand sneaks forward. Wrapping my fingers around it, I feel the give of the door as I gently turn the knob open. Before I get it too far, I look over at Periwinkle in time to see a tear slide down his cheek and onto his jacket. "What's wrong?"

"You have grown up so fast," Periwinkle replies, pulling out a hankerchief before wiping his eyes.

"Will I still see you?" I ask.

"Stop delaying and just open the door," Periwinkle replies.

I shake my head as I turn back to the door as my hand re-tightens around the bronze doorknob. As the door opens wider, the light erupts through the growing space, forcing Periwinkle to lower the rim of his hat over his eyes. Suddenly, I push the door open completely as the light engulfs me, blinding me from seeing anything around. As my forearm rises in order to shield some of the light, the light dims to reveal the space that stands in front of me.

Somehow, the darkness around me is gone and in its place is the setting of a book store, with books along every wall. In front of me, a single hallway takes shape between rows of empty shelves, except for the occasional cobwebs throughout. I stop myself from going forward and look back to see nothing but the backside of the door I had just seen in front of me. I then turn back to see the end of the rows as figures of various heights and weights rise up from the ground. One by one, they stand behind each other in a straight line in an awkward silence.

Curiously, I make my way forward as the sounds of whispers start to resonate around the room. Louder and louder the voices get, until finally I arrive at the side of the figures in front as they keep their attention toward a single direction. Remaining still, I watch as they sink back down into the ground almost as fast as they had risen. My eyes then turn to the right to see a table with two piles of book on both sides. Appearing to be the same book from top to bottom, I watch as they drop one by one. Behind the desk, a figure appears next to another in the shadows of the book shelving. I find myself staring face-to-face with an exact copy of Guillermo. Meanwhile, next to him, an inhuman creation manifests. Swelling up with cotton inside its body, golden fur covers up the pale skin as its face gains shape.

As its face grows roundish, bear-like attributes develop. Once the tail is in place, my eyes shift back to the human figure as he stands up from the desk. Not realizing it, my feet step forward to allow the desk to press up against my waist. I watch as the figure extends his hand out to me as his fingers take shape. Looking down, my own hand extends outward in order to meet just above the stacks of books. They wrap in a tight handshake, moving up and down as his hand releases mine.

"Enjoy," it says in a gurgling voice.

Looking down, I watch as he grabs one of the final two books remaining on the desk. He then lifts it up and places it inside my empty hand before stepping in front of the metal chair. Then before I can say something, the bearish figure stands up and places one of its pawlike appendages onto the human figure as they both stare at me. "Thank you."

They smile from behind a shadowy exterior when suddenly the lights go out in the room. My eyes struggle to find a source of light when suddenly the lights flicker back on, revealing a scene at the other end of the spectrum.

A room that is faintly lit, despite the fact that the large, brass windows let in all the sunlight without an ounce of resistance. Around me are circular tables, surrounded with chairs that have thick seats. My eyes shift all around at the wooden walls with hanging picture frames in different positions. My heart beats slowly as a feeling of despair and sadness swirls through the room. Suddenly, a whistling sound opens the door and shakes the items inside the room.

Looking all around, I continue to see nothing out of the ordinary, when something catches my eye as it rolls inside the room. To my surprise, the object was nothing more than a regular tumbleweed. Except, despite the gusty winds coming from the doorway, it rolls softly to a stop just feet from my shadow. Looking down at its thorny exterior, I kneel downward to get a closer look. My hands carefully extend forward in order to avoid the sharp objects along the stems curling together. That is when something catches my sight inside the core of this weed. Amber-orange with a white cap, my mind attempts to come up with a way to pull it out. Inspecting the thorny exterior, my eyes catch sight of an opening just large enough to stick my hand inside.

With a deep breath, my hand passes through without a prick or cut. Without any resistance, my hand arrives at the core as it wraps around the bottle stuck in the center. Then, carefully avoiding any traps on the way back, my hand pulls out the bottle as the remainder of the tumbleweed drops to the ground. Just as I attempt to examine the bottle, the tumbleweed unravels and it lays at full extension on the ground. I watch as it disintegrates into a fine black powder along the panel floor. Once the grains are small enough, the wind intensifies momentarily, causing the dust to swirl its way out the door.

Shaking my head, my eyes turn back to the amber bottle in my hand, catching sight of the moving liquid inside. It was bluish and appeared to be a water-like consistancy as it bounces around the container.

Catching sight of the white lid, I turn the top toward me and watch as the liquid settles back down to the bottom. As curiousity takes over, I place two fingers along it and attempt to try to spin it off. However, it stays in place, which causes me to get a second glance of the bottle. I wrap the the lid in my palm and push down as my index fingers pushes it to the side. Eureka, the top moves smoothly and suddenly the liquid inside starts to bubble. Tumbling and crashing around inside, the door of the room slams shut. My eyes shoot upwards when the frames comes tumbling down to the ground. Meanwhile, behind me, the walls close up, cutting the room in half as my hand drops off the bottle.

"What is going on here?" I say loudly.

Nothing and no one replies, instead smoke begins to appear inside the bottle as it begins to feel heavier in my grasp. Struggling to keep hold, the top shoots off the bottle and smashes into the tile along the roof. Before my eyes can make their way back down, something starts to rain down onto my fingers. Causing my grip to weaken, the bottle slips out of my fingers and lands on the floor. I watch as the liquid rushes out and onto the ground and suddenly rumbling sounds cause the room to vibrate. Intensifying, the liquid continues to spew from the bottle. The level falling, my eyes watch as the water continues to flow out. Then, before I can kneel down, the tiles along the roof explode downward, causing water to cascade down from the ceiling. As row by row explodes, my eyes look up as the last row remaining is the one going above my head.

"You might want to shield yourself," a voice whispers into my ear.

My knees sink to the ground as my arms lift above my head. Then, just as I get in place, the row of tiles above me erupt, sending the water crashing on top of me. Soaking me instantly, the water covers my face and eyes as I struggle to catch a breath. Unable to get a breath, my hands lower to my face and wipe away the water. Despite the continous flow, my mouth opens, allowing a water and air mixture inside. After spitting out the water, I take another breath as I struggle to take a step from out of the rising water. I make my way forward between two different rows of water. As it continues to approach my waist, the water steadily fills up the room and the tables begin to lift off the ground. Moving all about, the water decreases in intensity as the level stalls, my eyes meanwhile looking for an escape.

"I could use some help here!" I scream out into the room when suddenly the water stops all together.

"Will that suffice?" the voice replies back.

Trying to catch my breath, I watch as the water stiffens around me and the last few drops settle down. "Yes, but what am I supposed to take away from this?"

"That a mixture of water and faith that can bring forth a new version of you," the voice replies. The light from outside the window beams inward and aims its glow upon a metal chair that is struggling to hold itself in its position.

"What am I supposed to do?" I ask, keeping my eyes on the chair as it sway back and forth.

"Sit down," the voice replies.

Exhaling deeply, my nostrils flare as water falls off my face as I begin the trek toward the chair. Looking all around, the deep blue surface churns all around as objects float across the room. Continuing forward, the chair remains in place as I get closer, observing the area around me. Then, just as I am about to extend my hand forward, the chair snaps free from the ground and begins to float away.

"Oh no you don't," I say, reaching my hand out for the space between the metal headrest and the cushion along the back. As my fingers wrap around the metal, I grab hold of it and jam it back to the ground. Then, before the water can regain its hold, I place it underneath me and sit down upon the soggy cushion. My weight secures it to the ground and I look all around as I struggle to keep it in place.

"Take a deep breath," the voice speaks out.

I place my hand on both sides of the chair and plug my nose when suddenly I feel weights on both of my shoulders. Looking over each one, a single hand appears over each of my arms. On the left is a hand of brown color with not a scrape or cut, while on the ring finger is a band of rose gold with a sparkling item on the top. The hand on the right is completely different. It was a masculine hand with hairs sproadically about among the patches of black stains. Before I can identify either hand, they tighten their grasp on my skin and suddenly the chair starts to tilt upwards. Shifting my attention, my eyes watch as the water level approaches my head. As it comes closer, I shut my eyes, feeling the water overtake my entire body. Still feeling the tightness around my shoulders, the weight of the water lessens as the sunlight around me fades to darkness.

The darkness shifts back with a glimmer of light as the weight of the water disappears all together. Meanwhile, the fingers around my skin disappear as my hand frees my nose, revealing the fresh air waiting for my nostrils. Cautiously, I open my eyes to find myself in front of a tv screen on a channel swirling with static. Bouncing along the massive screen, the word *mute* in bright red letters goes back and forth. Looking left to right, my eyes take in the barely furnished room surrounded by plain white walls.

The patio door to my left stands tall in front of a flimsy futon, which sits next to my curvy chair. As my eyes proceed around, they find a coffee table with four glass squares around a metal frame painted a wooden tone. Continuing, my eyes see nothing beyond the beige carpet until I catch sight of a table with four chairs. The table, as high as my chest, sits in front of the wall by the kitchen as four chairs without a back sit on each side.

That's when my eyes catch sight of a reflection of light along the wall by the table. Unable to identify the source, my hands wrap around the cold metal handles and push me upwards. As the chair leans forward, my weight shifts to my feet, sending the chair back down. Turning my attention, my feet shift as I take my first steps toward the light. With each step, my eyes lock on the square of light, when suddenly a computer monitor appears on the table. Appearing to be the source, my eyes shift over to the white screen as a thin, black line flickers on and off. Then suddenly, I watch as the word *sacrifice* makes its way on the screen, with a period sitting at the end of it.

"Sacrifice?" I murmur.

"Something every writer has done for their craft," a voice says from out of nowhere.

My eyes bolting around the room, widen as they spot a human-sized clock sitting on the old futon mattress. "Who are you?"

"I have no name, I am simply just a tool to assist the writer," the clock replies.

"Assist who?" I ask.

"Him, by the table," the clock replies as the smaller of the two hands shifts a bit along its face.

"There is no one here," I reply, turning my attention back when I step back in shock.

Before my eyes, a male figure sits atop the stool between the table and the wall. His chest bare, his eyes remain fixed upon the screen before him. Meanwhile, his fingers press down upon the various keys on the keyboard. As line after line of jumbled words appear on the screen, I cautiously step closer to further examine the being. His face is unshaven and pale as the wall stays partially lit from the screen in front of him.

"He has been sitting there since before the beginning of my time," the clock says.

My eyes remain fixed on the man when he stops writing and looks over to the edge of the table. Awaiting him is a cheap, plastic cup with a brownish liquid inside, along with a single ice cube. He reaches over and grabs hold of it before bringing it over to his cracking lips. Placing it in front of his mouth, the writer slurps down a gulp before placing it back down alongside his screen. He then wipes his lips clear of any remnants of liquid and he returns his hands to the keyboard. "What is he doing?"

"Writing," the clock replies.

"I see that. So why am I here?" I ask, looking back over my shoulder to see the clock still sitting on the futon.

"Come over here and I'll show you," the clock replies.

I give the man a second look before turning away as I head over to the chair by the clock. Taking a seat, I watch as the clock grabs a remote off of the table and hands it over to me. "What do you want me to do with this?"

"Turn to the Sacrifice channel," the clock replies.

My eyes turn to the remote in search of the channel button when suddenly a pair of bright yellow arrows catch my sight. Finding one pointed up while the other faces down, my fingers aim for the one on top. As my finger pushes it downward, the silvery screen turns black and then back to static once again.

"Next one," the clock says.

Once again, my finger pushes down, which changes the screen to black, except this time it remained black with the word *sacrifice* in the top left corner. Before long, two words in blue lettering type on the screen as my eyes struggle to make them out from the dark background. "Sacrificial Things."

"Number one is Time," the clock says.

I then watch as the word *time* appears on the line beneath the other words. "What is next?"

"Number two is Money," the clock continues.

Once again, I watch as the word *money* appears on the line beneath time. "Wait, how does he sacrifice money?"

"By using it to give him the resources to not only edit his works, but to publish them as well," the clock replies.

"Got it," I reply, turning back to the screen.

"Finally, number three is Effort," the clock replies.

As my eyes turn to the line beneath the word *money*, the word *effort* appears letter by letter. "This may seem silly, but how does he sacrifice effort?"

"By sacrificing energy and ability to hone his craft as a writer," the clock replies, causing me to look over at the man by the table.

Continuing on, I watch as his fingers continue to click away until suddenly they stop. He sits up straight as he turns to me, revealing Guillermo's face as I look over to the clock. Except as my eyes look over, the clock is no longer in the room and the futon is gone, along with the remaining pieces of furniture, leaving nothing but myself and the author still sitting at his table. As I pick myself up off the floor, I look over, finding him still staring in my direction. Before I can say anything, he gets up from the table as it dissipates behind him. Once the final particle is out of the room, the two of us are left when the blinds on the three windows swing open. Turning my attention momentarily, the door to the apartment swings inward and a warm breeze fills the room.

"You coming, son?" a deep voice bellows from outside the open door.

My eyes turn back, catching the figure's movement as he makes his way to the door. After stepping from off the carpet and onto the pavement, he stops and looks back into the room. I watch as he scans the room one last time before turning back to face the outside light. Before I can watch him walk away, the door between us shuts and allows me to hear his faint footsteps. Growing weaker, his steps fade into silence as I settle inside my surroundings. Taking in the room, the computer screen on the table lights up, causing me to pause as it reflects off the wall.

"Go and read it," a voice says.

Without hesitation, I make my way to the stool and turn to the screen, looking at the word written on it. "Belief."

Just as the word escapes from my lips, the doorknob twists and the door pops open. My eyes look back, catching sight of the figure returning inside before doing another scan of the room.

"What did you forget?" the deep voice asks, echoing from outside the hall.

"I forgot one of the stools," the figure replies.

I then watch as the stool in front of me disappears, along with the computer. I step back when suddenly the entire table evaporates. The room is completely empty now and the figure steps back out of the doorway as the door closes in front of him. Alone once more, I look all around the room before making my way back to the living room. Once there, I walk over to the window all the way to the left, peeling open the blinds to get a look outside.

Before my eyes, an asphalt street separates the building from the next one right across from us. Sporadically placed, trees grow along the grass as the leaves flutter in the breeze. Cars of different colors are parked between the yellow lines on the opposite side of the trees. I step back as the blinds return to place when suddenly a crash echoes through the room.

Cautiously making my way to the opposite end, my eyes catch sight of the flickering lights above the hall to the left. Underneath, the metal cover from the air conditioner vent lays flat along the wooden panels. Stepping over, my eyes take in the area as I find myself at a fork with an open door on both sides. To the right, faint lights show a sink with a closet to the right. On the left, open space sits with strips of light bouncing off the carpet on the floor.

"Go inside," the voice replies.

"Which doorway?" I ask, looking around the empty space around me.

"The left side will take you on to the ending," the voice replies.

My eyes shift back to the left as my feet shift along the floor. I take my first steps to the room, approaching the doorframe as it reveals more of the room. Inside the room is emptiness as far as the surrounding walls with a few marks of discoloration. Orange specks line the wall close to me as black scratches carve their way onto the ones at the far end. Four indentations sit in the carpet as the rest of the room remains vacant. "There is nothing here."

"Step inside," the voice says.

Before I can step through, the image in the doorway ripples about, sending me back a step as I watch it stabilize. My eyes focus back on the image and I step toward the image as another ripple shoots from out of the bottom. This time, I continue forward as it dissipates at the top as I arrive at the doorway. After taking a deep breath, I step through the image with little resistance as my eyes shut. As my feet step down onto a moving surface, my eyes reopen to find myself back outside.

My eyes look down to see the fabric of Guillermo's shirt as it drops down toward his arms. Looking back, a wall of hair stops just shy of his shirt with a layer of skin separating the two. Over to the left, his ear casts a shadow along the space behind me. "I'm back where I started."

"Its about time, too," a familiar voice replies.

My eyes look around when I spot a shadow along the side of

Guillermo's hair. Turning around toward his shoulder, I find Periwinkle in his bright colors waving his hand back and forth. "What are you doing out here?"

"You are forgetting the best part of all heroic journeys," Periwinkle replies, lifting his hat off of his head.

"What's that?" I ask, watching as he places the hat down onto the fabric.

Periwinkle kneels down and looks over at me as I remain frozen in the shadows of Guillermo's ear. "The acknowledgement of success for a happy ending."

Before I can reply, feathers explode from out of the hat and onto the fabric beside it. Once the final feather is flat upon the pile, they start to spin rapidly until they shoot upwards into the sky. As my eyes struggle to keep track, the feathers come together into a single shadow, which grows larger on the way back. Getting closer, two wings sprout out from the sides, forming into a crow that I had seen before.

"Remember Edalpo?" Periwinkle says. He then lands onto one of the folds of the shirt as he points his golden beak at me.

"Yes, from the first ring," I reply, watching as Edalpo looks over at Periwinkle before turning back to me.

"Indeed," Edalpo caws.

"Still as simple as ever," I reply. I watch as Periwinkle smirks as Edalpo flaps his wings before settling back down.

"Just wanted to say, I hope you had a grand adventure of imagination," Edalpo replies.

"I did, and I learned a lot about the process of writing," I reply.

"A lot goes into it," Periwinkle says, when the ground beneath us shifts forward as Guillermo moves his arm.

"What is he writing?" I ask, following his arm down to his hand, which sits on top of the table. As my eyes lift up from his moving hand, they find a bright screen where lines of letters build up to rows of words.

"His next story," Periwinkle replies.

Before either of us can reply, Edalpo lifts off and lands down onto the edge of Guillermo's ear as he faces the screen.

I then watch as Periwinkle grabs the rim of his hat and then places it back onto his head. Once steady, Periwinkle makes his way over to the edge of his shoulder and sits down. With his legs laying flat against Guillermo's shirt, he turns to me as I remain in the shadows of his ear.

"Are you coming?" Periwinkle asks, tapping down on the fabric next to him.

Nodding my head, I make my way over to the edge of his shoulder, turning my attention to see the writing as, with each click, a letter appears on the screen. My eyes shift to the fabric beneath me as I squat down next to Periwinkle. Once comfortable, I turn my attention back to Periwinkle who keeps his eyes forward. "I do have one last question."

"What is it?" Periwinkle replies, looking over at me.

"If you are here, then who is leading the Imagination Circus?" I ask.

"About some time after you left, some strange character walked up and said he was my relief," Periwinkle replies.

"Seriously?" I reply.

"Maybe. Or maybe I will leave you in suspense until the sequel," Periwinkle replies.

"What's a sequel?"

"It's when a story is so good that you feel like another story is needed," Periwinkle replies.

"Do you think he will come up with a sequel?" I reply, turning my attention to Guillermo.

"Maybe after he finishes with this current story," Periwinkle replies.

"What is this one about?" I reply, trying to get a clearer view of the words on the screen.

"Talking animals, I think," Edalpo answers, causing us to turn our attention to him. Keeping his beak straight, his eyes wanders over to us before turning back to the screen in front of him.

"That's different," replies Periwinkle, turning his attention back to the screen.

As I watch their attention focus onto the screen, I shift my attention and watch as Guillermo continues to type away.

And the rest is history.

135

Reviews are crucial to indie authors like me. If you enjoyed this book, please leave me a review! It helps me and it helps others find my book, too! Thank you!

Also, check out my other books:

The Adventures of George and Reggie

The Adventures of George and Reggie 2: KING ORCAN'S REVENGE

Murdio

BloodMinazue

9 781087 841632